UNBROKEN

GLADYS ADISA ERUDE

Worlds Unknown Publishers

ISBN: 978-1-7356327-6-6 (Paperback)
ISBN: 978-1-7356327-8-0 (E-book)

Printed in the United States of America.
First printed edition 2020.

www.wupubs.com

Kavosa sat down by the roadside, her broken arm dangling by the skin, unable to cry. The pain was excruciating, and the cause of the pain was even more painful. She was in Jericho Estate, Nairobi, surrounded by idle people. Anything happening, no matter how small, attracted throngs of spectators. However, this was no small matter. People had been lynched for less. It was called "mob justice"—the only kind of justice that the people who meted it out knew.

The crowd shifted and milled around, people standing on tiptoe, shoving and pushing to get a better view of what was happening. The creative ones were already coming up with, and passing around different versions of what had happened in whispers and murmurs, punctuated by exclamations of sympathy and surprise.

"She's so old . . . who would want to do this to her?" a tall dark lady asked her neighbor through the fanned-out fingers of the hand she had put over her mouth.

"*Gai!*" gasped her shorter companion as she tightened the cotton lapper over her black tights. "Don't people fear curses?"

Kavosa's breathing was coming in long drawn gusts as she struggled with the pain. She was in no position to explain what had happened or even hear what the people around her were saying.

"Help me hold her arm," said Omanga, a portly man that worked at a hospital. Two middle-age ladies moved closer to help him administer first aid. He had fashioned a crude splint out of three thin pieces of wood. He tied the broken arm using strips of cloth torn from the *lesso* that Kavosa had been wearing. The splint would help to hold the pieces of fractured bone together and prevent further pain and injury while she was being rushed to Jericho Dispensary for more first aid before she could be taken to Kenyatta national Hospital, for that was certainly where she was headed

Kavosa was a soggy, bloodied mess . . . broken in body and spirit; a pathetic sight, huddled in her torn and shredded blood-soaked dress. From time to time, a low moan escaped her lips. Pain and suffering was a long-time acquaintance of hers; a companion she had had for the better part of her life.

1

Kavosa's entire life had been a rollercoaster ride, but she had survived it all. She was born at the time when boys were treasured more than girls. Girls were only tolerated because they would get married and bring in cows in the form of a dowry. Kavosa's mother had only three children. Again, at the time, people valued larger families because childhood mortality was high. People would typically have many children so that should some die, others would remain. But Kavosa's mother was unable to have more children, and so her father married another wife to give him more children.

One of her two brothers died in childhood, but one survived. He was later taken to enrolled in school because he was a boy. Kavosa went as far as class three in school, at which point her parents withdrew her, saying girls didn't need to go to school to learn how to hold a cooking stick.

Kavosa was smart—even smarter than her brother—and would have gone far had she been given a chance . . . but she was a woman! Although she dropped out of school after class three, she could read and write letters in vernacular. She would at times regret that she hadn't been allowed to continue with school, as one of her main goals was to be able to speak English. She later came to pick a few English words later in life.

Kavosa was much loved around Gaago village. She was the hardworking daughter everyone wanted. All her regular chores were as easy as a drink of water to her; farm work, fetching firewood and water . . . she even willingly volunteered to do these chores for the old and otherwise incapacitated people around the village when she was done doing them for her mother.

Her mother was frail and sickly. Kavosa loved her so much and did everything to make her comfortable. Although she loved her father as well, she feared him because he was violent, especially after consuming *busaa*. She also resented him for mainly favoring his second wife and her children, and hardly ever coming to their hut.

Kavosa's mother succumbed to her ailment eventually, which was later suspected to have been breast cancer. It all started after giving birth to her late son, who died in childhood. Her left breast got so swollen that she couldn't feed the baby on that side. Even the village herbalist, who was well known for his herbs that cured all ailments, including malaria and stomach troubles, was unable to cure her. Herbal medicine was all they could turn to then. Hospitals then were few and often situated long distances away, and often did not have qualified personnel or drugs.

Despite the ministrations of the herbalists, the illness progressed until the entire side of her chest was just one big wound that oozed bloody puss. She was in excruciating pain, until her death three years later. Apart from her swollen breast, she also had incessant migraines.

As a last resort, her last treatment involved making an incision at the nape of the head. Then, with a small tin, the herbalist set a small piece of paper on fire, inserted it in the small tin, and covered the incision with the tin. The tin would stick to the head, and then the herbalist would pull it forcefully, sucking the blood out of the head through the incision. This was a traditional Maragoli way of releasing tension that caused headaches. But even that didn't cure Kavosa's mother. Kavosa was only sixteen years old when her mother died, and she was totally devastated.

With her father permanently in the other house, she remained all alone in her late mother's house. Her elder brother had long gone to Nairobi in search of a job after completing Class Eight. He only came home to his mother's burial, after which he took a wife from the village and went back to Nairobi.

Kavosa was too scared to sleep alone in her mother's house after she died. After all, the Maragoli believed that the dead came back to visit their homes at least once after their burial in the dead of night.

The culmination of the burial rites was the hair-shaving ceremony. All close relatives of the departed—men, women and children—were required to completely shave their heads clean. After this, all of them left the home. They had come from far and wide- some from as far as South Nyanza where they had settled in the search for farming land. By the time the last relatives left, Kavosa had made arrangements with her friends Makungu and Vuhya to keeping her company at night.

The three friends became very close, doing all the chores together. They would till each other's land in turns, fetch water together, and also go places, like the posho mill. The only posho mill was in Lusiola, a distance of about three miles from Gaago village. It was also an uphill task to climb from Gaago to Lusiola, but going back was easier.

The three girls had become inseparable. At least that's what they thought until one fateful day. It happened during one of their trips to the posho mill at Lusiola. The three girls met a group of twelve boys. They knew they were twelve because as they approached the group, the boys divided themselves into three groups of fours. They had obviously carefully planned it. Apparently, unbeknown to her, this was to be her wedding day.

It turned out that the boys had for a long time been watching the three girls together and planned to waylay them so they could marry them. That is how it used to be done. The boys were in their early twenties and much stronger than the girls. Each group of four grabbed a girl each and carried each one of them shoulder high, as some of the boys hauled the flour they had just milled.

"You are now getting married," was all they tersely said to the girls. Makungu was taken to Vigeze village, Vuhya was taken to Vigina Village, and Kavosa was taken by a boy called Musoda from Masizi village on the banks of the Lusavasavi River.

Word had gone round that the three girls of Gaago village had been caught and married off. It was a normal incident that happened all the time, and so the mothers only waited to see who had taken their daughters. The following day, as was the custom, a woman would be given whatever the girl was carrying to take to their homes and inform the parents where their daughter was.

While Makungu and Vuhya's flour was taken to their mothers, Kavosa did not have a mother, so the messenger traveled to her stepmother's hut and informed the family. Her stepmother thought it good riddance, as she had been coveting Kavosa's house for a long time. Kavosa had seven stepbrothers and one sister. All those children were malnourished because their mother was lazy while the father was old and drank too much.

Upon hearing that kavosa was now married, Kavosa's father was excited because he knew he was about to get cows in the form of dowry. He informed the messenger to go back and report that he was in agreement with the marriage. He wanted to know when he could go and negotiate the dowry, even before he knew if his daughter was happy or not. She was just a girl. What she thought and wanted didn't matter.

There was something else the woman who brought the flour to Kavosa's home brought with her. It was a bloody old blanket that Kavosa and her new husband had used that night. It was bloody because Kavosa had known no other man. She'd been a virgin. Tradition demanded that the beddings used in the first night be sent back to the girl's home. There was a sense of pride to know that one raised a well-behaved, virgin daughter. The beddings would normally be given to a grandmother or any old woman who had stopped having children, according to the Maragoli tradition. In Kavosa's case, it was all a waste because her mother was gone, and there really was no one to take genuine pride in her condition— except, perhaps, for her grandmother. Her father was happy but only because the bloodied blanket meant he was going to be given a goat as "compensation" for his daughter's virginity. That was the value of virginity.

2

Kavosa started off her marriage traumatized and in a panic. She had been forcefully carried to a village she didn't like, and she wasn't sure what to expect. She had lost her voice from screaming and was sore all over from fighting the men that were too strong for her. The more she struggled, the tighter the men gripped her. The onlookers they passed only laughed with amusement. Kavosa had hoped someone would come to her rescue. But no wrong had been done in the eyes of her society. Even the chief himself—the person that crimes were reported to locally—had acquired his wife the same way.

The men took Kavosa to a small, round grass-thatched hut that was going to be her new home. On the bed was one single blanket, and it had a mat made of papyrus reeds for a mattress. On the other side of the hut was a three-stoned hearth where food was cooked, but since the man was not married at the time, he used to get his meals from his mother's house.

Maragoli men traditionally could not cook or fetch water. That was the work of women and girls. Before marriage, a young man would typically have his sisters do everything for him. So that night, Musola's sister brought food for two. Musoda had told them that he had a visitor. That was enough for his mother to conclude that he had brought home somebody's daughter. Moreover, his mother had heard the commotion and knew something was going on. It was a subject they had discussed before, with his mother pushing him to marry so she could have somebody to help her with home chores.

Since it was seven o'clock when they arrived, Musoda had to fetch his *koroboi*, a small tin lamp with a piece of cloth for a wick. In the hut was also a small table made from the same material as the bed. Posts were fixed on the floor with sticks arranged to form a surface that could hold plates.

Musoda was a dark, short and well-built young man. He could handle any physically demanding job. Neighbors hired him to do heavy menial work because of his physical strength. He had very strong legs—probably developed when he used to play soccer for his primary school. He quit school at Class Four. Although his mother would have done anything to educate him, Musoda was unable to pass the Common Entrance Examination, or CEE. This was a standardized exam taken nationally in Class Four. One had to pass it to join Intermediate School, but Musoda hadn't. He'd been allowed to repeat several years, due to the fact that he was a good soccer player for the school, but he finally gave up after the fifth trial.

Musoda's mother had made a special dish of *ugali* with chicken stew for the visitor Musoda had brought home. Kavosa was still sobbing, wondering how she would start life with a man whose name she didn't even know. She knew it was impossible to go back home after spending a night with a man in his hut. Any girl who did that acquired the derogatory label *kidwaadi*, which marked them as spoilt goods. It would be difficult to find a marriage partner. Her only options would be to marry a widower, or become a second or third wife to a much older man.

That night, Musoda raped Kavosa—technically. Kavosa resented Musoda, and not just because he raped her that first night. His body smelled of sweat. He didn't not wear shoes, and so his feet were calloused. The only shoes he wore were *akala*, sandals made from old car tyres. His only shirt was torn at the shoulders. He washed it once a week at night and would wear it in the morning even if it wasn't completely dry.

Kavosa shuddered at the touch of his rough and calloused hands. That didn't deter Musoda from achieving his goal of consummating his marriage that first night and making Kavosa his wife. He succeeded after a long struggle, and it was excruciating for Kavosa.

Kavosa got some sleep because she was exhausted. The bed was hard and uncomfortable, but she was used to sleeping on the floor on a papyrus mat even at her mother's house. That was the way of all girls. Boys made themselves a rough bed similar to Musoda's, but the mat still made the mattress.

As she slept, Kavosa had a dream in which she saw her mother trying to rescue her from an ogre. The ogre was huge, and her mother was too frail to help. She got up with a start as soon as the ogre carried her off on its back, running to the forest. She was thankful that it had only been a dream, but then she felt Musoda's arm around her.

She tried to wriggle out of the embrace, but that woke Musoda up. That is the time he asked her what her name was and where she came from. Musoda said he had been watching her and had enquired about her and knew that they were not related at all. She was from the Avaguuga clan while Musoda came from Avafunami clan. Musoda's mother was from Avamigango clan while Kavosa's mother was from Avamuluga clan. That said, it was clear that there was no relationship between them. Marriage between members of the same clan was forbidden

Kavosa asked to use the bathroom and was shown a pit latrine with wall made of dry maize stalks. She tried to stand and found it difficult to walk. It took her a long time to get to the latrine behind the hut. Musoda wasn't in the hut when she came back. He came in after a short while accompanied by his old grandmother. Once again, the grandmother greeted Kavosa and proceeded to the bed, from which she retrieved the only blanket. Having made sure that it had blood on it, she folded it and put it in a small bag. She asked Musoda to leave so she could talk to Kavosa. After Musoda left the hut, his grandmother started questioning Kavosa.

She wanted to know whose daughter she was and if she had ever known a man before her grandson. Kavosa shyly answered, "No." She quickly explained that it was imperative for her to know if the blood was a result of virginity or simply her monthly periods.

"Was this your time of the month?" she asked.

"No . . . it was not . . ." Kavosa fidgeted shyly as she answered.

The older woman explained that it would not be good on Kavosa's part if traditions were followed for the wrong reason. For example, there was the goat to be paid as compensation for a virgin and the blanket on which she bled had to be taken back to her home. Kavosa understood and confirmed that she was a virgin. This made the grandmother very happy.

Musola's grandmother then quickly made a fire and put on a pot of water to boil, adding some herbs to it. Some of the herbs had red sap, which made the water brownish in color. She filled a basin with the water and asked Kavosa to strip and sit in the basin with hot water. She tried to say that the water was too hot, but the grandmother told her it was good for her to clean and sanitize her womanhood so that it wouldn't become septic after forceful penetration.

While Kavosa was soaking in the herbal water, one of Musola's female relatives was summoned to was brought in to carry the flour Kavosa had the previous day, which was still sitting in a basket near the door of Musoda's hut. The messenger was also handed the soiled blanket and twenty shillings to take to Kavosa's grandmother and report that she was married and now belonged to the Avafunami clan.

The twenty shilling note and the blanket were given to Kavosa's blind grandmother, but the goat was for her father to slaughter on a chosen day and make a feast for the Avaguuga clan. The goat would be delivered after one week. The woman messenger was given chicken in gratitude for her service of delivering good news. She also brought back Kavosa's clothes, which consisted of an extra petticoat, and two extra pairs of underwear, unlike Musola, who only owned a single shirt.

Musoda's grandmother continued treating Kavosa every morning until she started getting used to the idea that she was married and had to be with her man, no matter how painful the exercise was. Musoda's grandmother was a very kind woman. She made Kavosa feel at home and that she could confide in her.

Exactly one week after being snatched, it was mandatory for Kavosa to go visit her home. Musoda's mother had tried to feed her well so that she could earn some points for being a good mother in law. At first, Kavosa had refused to eat, as was custom with newly married girls. Her new family implored her to eat, even offering her money, or a live chicken. Sometimes, girls who married into well-to-do families would demand a cow before they ate. Kavosa could not ask for much because she saw the home was a humble one. The only blanket Musoda owned had to be taken to Kavosa's home, and so the grandmother offered them one of hers. Musoda's aunt, worked for a white person in Nairobi and once in a while would bring home blankets.

After about a week, Kavosa had began putting on a little weight. She was used to working while she was still at her mother's house, but during this one week, she just ate and rested. She was still recuperating from the ordeal. Also, newlyweds weren't supposed to do anything until they paid a visit to their homes after one week. Her father was happy, and the neighbors even envied her. Because they were married on the same day, Kavosa reunited with her two friends as they were also visiting their homes for the first time since they were abducted. That was the first time they found out where each of them had been married off to.

Kavosa was accompanied by her sister-in-law. After the visit, they were given a *kihinda* full of sorghum flour, some beef, and a cockerel to take back to their homes. Eager to cash in on his good fortune as soon as possible, Kavosa's father sent them with a letter asking when he would visit the home to discuss what he would receive as his daughter's dowry.

3

Kavosa returned from her home visit to Masizi village with flour, two kilograms of beef, and a cockerel signified that the relationships between the two families—as a matter of fact, the two clans of *Avaguuga* and *Avafunami*—had been sealed. At only sixteen, going on to seventeen, she was expected to behave as a wife, a daughter-in-law, and a sister-in-law. As if that wasn't enough, the whole village was keen to see how the *mwiha*, or newly married girl, was behaving.

Her duty from now henceforth was to get up at dawn, sweep her hut, and sweep her mother-in-law's hut too. She would also need to scoop cow dung from the shed, where the two cows in the family were tethered for the night. The homestead had two goats, but one had to be surrendered to Kavosa's father after she was found to be a virgin. She would then grab a pot and walk downstream to fetch water, balancing the full pot of water on her head on the walk back. She would them make breakfast for the family, which was mainly sour porridge or sometimes tea, if they had enough money for sugar. She was used to doing chores like these since she was raised with an ailing mother and had to do most daily chores.

After breakfast, she was expected to go to the farm to dig or cultivate some crops. It was also her duty to find grass for the cows and one goat, and also drive the animals to the stream to drink. Since Kavosa started doing chores in the home, it seemed as though everybody stopped what they used to do because she was there.

Musoda's mother left everything to concentrate on her pottery. She used to make pots out of clay, dry them in the sun, and then bake them, testing the perfection of the pot by tapping it gently with a stick. The sound it gave showed how well it was baked. She would then pile the baked pots in a long line separated by banana leaves, then tie them together like beads on a string. She then walked the six kilometres to Kiboswa Market to sell them. Kavosa recognized the path that passed near her house. It was the one she used to take with her mother to the market. Her mother, too, had been a potter.

Kavosa was happy that her mother-in-law was a potter just like her late mother. Kavosa attached herself to this mother—first because she missed having a female mentor since her mother died but also because it was imperative to love and work together with one's mother-in-law. She helped to fetch clay and knead it before her mother-in-law embarked on the pottery work. It was time-consuming but Kavosa enjoyed it.

That was her daily life for a month. She was beginning to get used to her husband's sweaty smell and rough hands. She even started developing a liking for him and looked forward to Musoda's return home from where he went to do menial jobs to bring in money for food. She would run his bath by boiling water and carrying it in a basin to the ramshackle bathroom.

Musoda actually loved her, and he was the envy of other boys in the village. He had managed to bring home a beautiful girl—slender and chocolate-colored with shapely legs. The Maragoli were partial to women with big legs. She had naturally white teeth with a gap between her front two. To crown it all, she had dimples in both her cheeks. She merited every description of a beautiful girl in the Maragoli community. Her hair was short, cut with a pair of scissors, and trimmed all around with a razor, in a style called *mugungu*.

Kavosa was always quick to finish her tasks so she could have time to sit and rest, but her mother-in-law would always come up with another task to be done. Sometimes she ask her to grind sorghum mixed with millet and dried cassava on the *lugina*, which was a large rock with a flat surface. A smaller round stone, rounded on top and flat and smooth underneath, called an *ihyu*, was used to grind the grain on the larger rock. It was an exquisite skill that every mother was expected to teach her daughter.

Only maize could be taken to the posho mill. The Maragoli believed taking sorghum to the posho mill meant nutrients being blown away, leaving only the bran. They therefore ground sorghum by hand. Kavosa could not say she didn't like the idea, but saying "no" to a parent-in-law was taboo. As much as she dreaded it, she still did it.

Six weeks after Kavosa's marriage to Musoda, she became sick. She believed it was malaria since it was a rainy season and the maize crop in the farms was beginning to ripen for harvest. Everybody believed that the green maize caused the malaria, and thus they cautioned their children not to eat it. They also believed malaria as not a disease to write home about. It was rampant.

If a child was down with malaria, he or she would stay home, lying on a mat under a tree or the eaves of the house, with a large bowl of water. Throwing up the greenish-yellow bile juice was a sign that the malaria was getting out of the system. Sometimes, people threw up until they became severely dehydrated and died, but the relatives would refuse to believe that it was malaria that claimed their loved-one's life. Those who could afford it took their patients to the single doctor in Maragoliland, a man named Henry Mboku who operated a clinic in Gambogi. He only charged two shillings a visit.

Kavosa became so sick that nothing went into her mouth before coming out faster than it went in. Once again, it was Musoda's grandmother who came to interrogate her, and she soon discovered that Kavosa was pregnant. She said that it had been her prayer that Kavosa conceived. "Pure girls like you don't take long to get pregnant. God is good," she said.

After his grandmother's declaration, Musoda took it upon himself to do the chores his wife did. This did not go well with the villagers. "Does he think he married a Mzungu?" one was heard thinking aloud." Musoda will make all women in this village grow big heads," quipped another one. But Musoda didn't pay them any mind.

He had come to love Kavosa immensely. She had even gone to Majengo market and bought him a second-hand shirt and a pair of shorts. "Thank you, my wife, for taking care of me. Nobody has ever treated me this way since the death of my father fifteen years ago," he had said emotionally as tears rolled down his face. He let his emotions out, despite this being culturally considered a sign of weakness, as men were not allowed to cry before women. Now that it was his turn to take care of Kavosa, he did it wholeheartedly.

Musoda had recalled how his father used to go places with him. He died when Musoda was only eight years old. Masizi village was situated on the seasonal Lusavasavi River. When it rained, it flooded and even caused soil erosion to people's farms, Musoda's included. There was no bridge to cross the river, but two large trees had been felled and put across the water to act as a bridge.

It was one of those days when Musoda's father had gone to work in Logere, a village on the other side of the river. On coming back home, he could not see the logs that had been the bridge. He attempted to cross where he thought the makeshift bridge was, but he was pulled in by the current and swept away. He tried to stay afloat but was overpowered.

The angry river spat out his dead body three miles downstream. As soon as his body was found, the villagers made a raft on which to carry it back home. Such a death was taboo according to Maragoli culture. People who met their deaths that way were not supposed to be mourned but buried as soon as possible.

While some people went to bring back the body, others stayed behind to dig the grave. The village elders from the clan silenced the crowd as they lowered the body into the grave and covered it. The grave was also leveled and not shaped into a mound, as would the grave of a person that had met a natural death. It was after the un-ceremonial burial that people were allowed to wail.

It still hurt Musoda that his dad left him at a very tender age—and also that the custom had prevented them from mourning him, as if he had chosen to die that way. He felt sad that he never had the chance to talk to him one last time, let alone viewing his body in death. Musoda lamented that if his father were alive, he would build him a better hut than the one he had.

He had been a builder, and most houses in their village were credited to his expertise.

"When he had money after being paid dues from his work, he bought me clothes. He was planning to teach me the profession of building houses when I grew up, but now here I am," he concluded bitterly.

Kavosa listened sympathetically, recalling her own mother's death, and having been left all alone because her father lived with her stepmother who didn't like Kavosa. Although she had been abducted forcefully and made to marry somebody whose name she didn't even know, she was now glad that she had company.

As her pregnancy progressed, Kavosa remembered that the ailment her mother had succumbed to had started with a simple pregnancy. She thought of how her mother used to send her for different fruits like guavas and mangoes but she wouldn't eat them. She would ask for porridge, and Kavosa would hurry to prepare it only for her to say she didn't want it. "Am I going to die like my mother with this pregnancy?" she asked nobody in particular. But she again thought of the joy of having her own child that resembled her—like her neighbor's child, whom she used to babysit. She longed for someone to love and protect from every danger.

She couldn't even imagine sending her to the posho mill lest something befalls her like it happened to her. A strange thing was that she thought about her baby in terms of a baby girl. She never wanted a boy who would most likely end up being like her rowdy step-brothers. They stole from neighbors' farms and houses, their language was foul, and they would start fights with anybody. They even stole onions, tomatoes, and pumpkins from farms. They didn't care that it was taboo to steal eggs and pumpkins because it was believed to cause deaths as the thief's stomach would swell and burst, killing him instantly.

"Why doesn't their mother do anything?" she used to wonder. She knew her father was not much of a disciplinarian. Her late mother had been the strict one. And now her father seemed to be living in fear of his wife.

When Kavosa's pregnancy was at three months, she slowly started regaining her normal self. She threw up less and at least ate a little. Her husband was happy and tried to provide anything she wanted that he could afford. Her mother-in-law was supportive, advising her to get up early and do some chores. She insisted that doing chores that exercising the baby made delivery easier. Indeed, there were women who were nine months pregnant but would fetch water and firewood, go to work on the farm, come home, and prepare supper for the family, only to deliver a baby in the night.

Kavosa hoped she would be one of such women. She was strong enough. And she tried her level best to be active so that her delivery would be easy. She didn't know what to expect.

4

One fine evening Musoda came home excited, saying he had met his two friends—the two who married Vuhya and Makungu on the same day Kavosa was taken to Musoda's hut. These two friends were better off than Musoda, although they had been friends from childhood and went to the same school. Their names were Silingi and Kiyundi. The two friends had passed their Common Entrance Examination after two unsuccessful attempts and proceeded to Gavalagi Intermediate School. They had, however, dropped out of school in Class Six because the teachers were beating them severely.

When a recruiter came to the village seeking to find people to take to pick tea at Kericho Tea Plantations, Silingi and Kiyundi jumped at the chance. They lived in Kericho and came home well-dressed. They even had real shoes, not *akala*, which almost everyone wore. They had come to the village to find wives that they could take back to Kericho. Their boss had advised them to have wives because of the nature of their jobs they were dealing with foodstuff and were not expected to get sexually transmitted diseases—which they were less likely to get if attached to a spouse. Furthermore, being married entitled them to company living quarters.

Makungu and Vuhya therefore had a more economically stable start. They moved to Kericho immediately after they got married. Now they were back in the village, since both were on vacation from work. Silingi and Kiyundi convinced their friend Musoda to go back with them so he could get a job like theirs and come back to take Kavosa with him. The thought of living with Kavosa in town excited Musoda. "I would be able to buy you new clothes, and our unborn child would have a better life if I had I job," he announced to Kavosa.

Kavosa had grown attached to Musoda so much that she feared being left alone by a loved one just like her mother had left her. But the thought of being reunited with her friends in town was more enticing. She agreed. Musoda informed his mother of the impending travel. She was happy because she knew her son would be sending money back home. His grandmother blessed him by spitting on his forehead. Musoda would put up with his friends, and after he earned his first salary, he would move into his own house. Then he would have Kavosa move in with him.

Before he left, he made arrangements that his sister, who was ten years old, would keep Kavosa company. Yes, Musoda's sister was ten because after his father died, his mother was given a man from the clan to inherit her. The man was the father of the little girl. In this case, the children fathered by the inheritor belonged to the dead man. That's why Musoda confidently called Kadogo his sister.

Tradition demanded that your mother's husband become your father, and so Musoda called Kadogo's father "Baba" although he was his father's cousin, which technically made him Musoda's uncle. The Maragoli call their paternal uncles "father" and maternal aunties "mama." An uncle is the brother to your mother and an aunt is a sister to your father.

Getting wood for baking his mother's pots had been Musoda's duty, a fact that was now worrying the women in the homestead, now that he was leaving for Kericho. After the pots were baked, both women would trek all the way to Kiboswa and Mbale markets to sell them.

If the market was good and the pots sold successfully, Musoda's mother would give Kavosa a little pocket money. Kavosa didn't spend the money but saved it in a tin under her bed. She knew that when she got a baby, she would need to buy clothes for it. She couldn't buy a baby things before the baby was born because it was considered a bad omen. One had to hold the newborn baby in their arms before sending somebody to buy whatever was needed.

Kavosa was also happy that Musoda was going to Kericho to look for money so he could build a more spacious house than the hut they lived in, which was Musoda's *isimba*, a name given to a bachelor's hut. At the same time, men were not supposed to be near women who were giving birth. In fact, it was custom for a baby to take up to six months away from the marital bed with her husband. Some men wouldn't even hold their baby until it was at least three months old.

Nobody knew what would happen if they did, but it was taboo for men to do women's work. So, Kavosa was happy because she had reasons for desiring her husband to be away when she had the baby. But she still cried and clung to him the morning he was leaving.

Musoda and his friends were scheduled to leave on a Saturday morning. They chose Saturday because it was a busy day, and transport to and from the market was available.

Kavosa escorted him up to Majengo, where he linked up with his friends. They took a bus to Kisumu, where they could get another bus to take them to Kericho. They needed a day for Musoda to rest and see places before he started work on Monday. The friends had secured a place for him to join them in picking tea.

From Majengo, Musoda sat strategically at a window so he could wave at his wife as she waved back with teary eyes.

Kavosa walked back home, already missing him, but she consoled herself that it was for the better that they stay apart for a while.

5

Musoda had been in Kericho for six weeks without communication. He had not been paid yet, and so he couldn't afford a stamp to send a letter home. The only reliable communication there was with distant loved ones was through mail. He yearned for Kavosa, but the need to get money to build a better life for her was stronger. He endured the hardships until he got his first pay.

He got his six hundred Kenyan shillings, which was much more than he had ever earned in his lifetime. He wrote a letter and sent it to Kavosa. He mailed it and enclosed a money order of two hundred shillings. The letter took two weeks to arrive at the destination. Kavosa didn't have a post office box, so she used the local school's address, like many other people did in the village.

The school's Headmaster, regularly lent his bicycle to one student, and sent him to Maragoli Post Office, Mbale. That was the only post office in Maragoli for a long time, until the services were diversified, bringing one to Majengo as well. In the evening after school, there would be a parade or assembly for those who had made mistakes to be punished—mistakes like speaking vernacular on the school compound. There was a small piece of wood called "the disc," which was given to anyone caught speaking vernacular. Whoever refused would get eight stokes of the cane, but those who took it and gave to others would get only two stokes of the cane. Girls would be caned on the palms of their hands while boys would get caned on their behinds.

Some boys would put books under their shorts so they didn't feel the pain. Whenever they got caught, the cane strokes would be doubled. Those who made noise in class and had their names written down prefects would also be revealed and punished at this time.

After the punishments had been meted, students and teachers would sing a hymn, and one of the teachers or a chosen student would say prayers. It was after prayers that the letters or mail would be read out aloud. Whoever knew the recipient would pick it up and send it to the owner. That's when the name Ronika Kavosa Musoda was read out. A student from Masizi village picked it up and made sure she delivered it to Kavosa. It's a good thing that most people were honest. Nobody opened another's letter. They made sure the letters were delivered in perfect condition.

Kavosa opened the letter and to her surprise, there were two pieces of paper in the envelope. The system of education when Kenya was still under the colonial rule was very good. Students dropping out of school in Class Three like Kavosa could read and write well. Kavosa did not need to find someone to read the letter for her. She thanked God for this, remembering the story her mother told her about a woman who walked the whole village, looking for somebody to read her letter. Some people who pretended to know how to read lied to her all the time, and she never knew the exact wording of the letter.

Musoda's letter to Kavosa was short. Living in Kericho within a multi-culture helped him pick up some English words, whose spelling in English he didn't know. He had barely started learning English but never passed the Common Entrance Examination to join Intermediate School where he could learn more English. The letter read:

Tu mayi diya Kavosa
I havu sendi yu samu mane bikosi I geti a jobu.
I misi yu vere machi.

(To my dear Kavosa, I have sent you some money because I got a job. I miss you very much.) He concluded the letter in vernacular with instructions to her to give his mother fifty of the two hundred shillings, and his grandmother twenty. When he got a chance he would visit soon, God willing.

Kavosa was very happy and re-read the letter at least twenty more times. That night, she put the letter under her head as she slept, lest it get lost. It was the first love letter Kavosa had ever received in her life. She borrowed a page from Kadogo's book to write a reply, so that when she went to the post office to cash her money order, she would mail the replies there and then.

She discussed the letter with her mother-in-law before leaving very early for Mbale. But first, she had to go through Assistant Chief's house, would provide her an identification letter, because at that time, women did not have identification cards. The assistant chief demanded two shillings but Kavosa promised to pay him as soon as she came back. Heavily pregnant as she was, she walked the six miles to Mbale.

Kavosa knew where the post office was because she used to see it whenever she would take pots to the market. On this day she was in Mbale for different reasons. She waited nervously in line, but when her turn to be served came, the teller was very helpful, and the letter from the assistant chief identified her fully.

The teller asked who had sent her the money, and she answered, "My husband." The teller asked who her husband was, and she proudly announced that it was Julius Musoda Asengi of Masizi village who now works at Kericho. That was more than enough information but it proved a point. She was given the two hundred shillings and asked to sign for it. She wrote her name. Leaving the post office, she was extra careful that no one knew she had money of that magnitude. She made sure to buy a pound of sugar, tea leaves, soap, salt, and a pound of beef. The total cost of those things was seventeen shillings. She had enough money left to take a bus home and still pay the assistant chief for his identification services.

Kavosa distributed the money as Musoda instructed her, and even gave Kadogo one shilling to buy a pencil or do whatever she so wanted. Pencils cost only ten cents. Kavosa was tired from the day's activities and excused herself to go to bed early. Her mother-in-law was happy and grateful for the items she had brought home. Food at the homestead was still prepared at mother-in-law's house. She did most of the cooking and just came to sleep in her hut.

When the time came for her to start cooking her own food, she would have to go to her father's home to get a cooking pot, a basket of flour (ideally sorghum), and a pound of meat and chicken. There would be a ceremony in which her sister or cousin-in-law would prepare the hearth for her, making a fire and heating water for the *ugali,* at which point Kavosa would finish the work. As people enjoyed the meal she prepared, they would pray for her to be blessed in in her house. But this could happen only when Musoda was around.

She knew she was almost due and that she could have her baby anytime, but she didn't know what to expect.

That night at around three o'clock she was woken up by a dull ache in her lower back. She thought she had walked too much that day and that she was just having the normal aches after a hard day's work. At seven o'clock she tried to get out of bed, but her legs were too heavy, and she was starting to have some bouts of pain in her lower abdomen. The back pain was also intensifying.

It was a Saturday morning and schools were not in session. She sent Kadogo to tell her mother that she was unwell. Her mother came running, wiping her hands on her dress. She asked what was wrong.

"I'm having this pain in my lower back and lower abdomen. I can't even get out of bed because my legs are heavy and painful. Maybe it's because I walked too much yesterday," she concluded. Her mother-in-law smiled, and Kavosa wondered why it amused her mother-in-law to hear that she was in pain. She excused herself and ran out to call the grandmother. Grandmother insisted that they call Femina, the village midwife.

In a short while, the three women came back with Femina clutching her paraphernalia that she used for midwifery. She asked Kavosa to try and lie on her back, then touched her stomach and massaged it, announcing that the baby was on its way and that it would be out in less than three hours' time. She took charge, ordering the other women around.

6

Femina sent Kavosa's mother-in-law to get banana leaves and make a bed on the floor. Next, they helped Kavosa out of bed and lay her on the fresh banana leaves. It was believed that banana leaves were fresh and sterile to welcome the newborn. In fact, if a woman had a pre-term baby that survived, it was held in young banana leaves until it grew. It was not bathed at all until the nine-month mark was reached.

Fresh banana leaves served as incubators, and somehow babies survived. Kavosa's baby, however, was full-term and ready to be born. After three hours of the painful agony of labor pains, Kavosa felt like she wanted to go to the toilet outside. "I want to go to the toilet" she begged, to which the women said that she was free to poop where she was and that they would be happy to clean it.

It was embarrassing but as the urge continued, Kavosa couldn't help it but poop in the house. She thought the poop was as hard as the last time she had been constipated. Surprisingly, the women were encouraging her to push the poop out. She pushed and pushed. Femina urged her with laughter in her voice to give it one more push. With one last mighty push, the poop was out—except there was a cry of a baby. "You did it!" the women said in unison. Surprised, Kavosa heard them happily exclaim that it was a girl.

"This is Iminza, Musoda's great grandmother!" said Grandma. Musoda's mother agreed with her, and so the name of the baby girl was known.

Femina continued pressing her belly gently until the placenta was expelled. After cleaning her up, grandma went to scoop cow urine from the cow shed. They washed their hands in the urine before rinsing them with soap and water. Cow urine was believed to be a good sterilizer at the time—especially in the villages where hospitals were unheard of. Wherever there appeared a stain of blood on the floor, grandma was quick to scoop ashes from the hearth and spread them over it, making it disappear.

This was an advantage of mud floors. Kavosa had gone through the episode of her labor with courage and without a teardrop. The older women had warned her not to scream or cry during child birth. According to tradition, the angel of death could take it to mean the mother hated the baby and steal it away. Truly, the pain of childbirth pain was severe, but Maragoli women, like the Hebrew women described in the bible, are very strong and courageous. They may moan and stretch but never scream or shed tears during labor. That's how they are socialized.

Kavosa was so happy to see her own baby girl. The women cleaned the bloody banana leaves and cut fresh ones, for that would be her bed for quite some time. For three months, Kavosa was not allowed to do any work. Her work was to bathe herself, give the baby a bath and breastfeed. Even her bath was warmed and taken to the bathroom by her mother-in-law. The diet at this juncture consisted of fermented sorghum porridge, some milky tea, and other nutritious foods. Nobody wanted her to break her back working, as bringing a baby into the world was a huge task. Like many other Maragoli women before her, Kavosa was given time to recuperate and heal adequately.

Musoda wasn't around but if he had been, he could have given money to his mother to buy the first baby blanket. This was a tradition to prove the baby belonged to the clan. Musoda's mother had to spend part of the fifty shillings she was given by Kavosa to buy the first baby clothes and blanket before she bought more with Kavosa's money.

The Maragoli are patriarchal. All children would therefore belong to the father. In case of divorce, which was very rare, the children stayed at their father's home. That was why the naming of the baby had to be done by Musoda's grandmother because she had stepped in for her husband to be the head of the family, as Musoda's father had also died.

The baby was three months old when Musoda finally wrote a letter to say he was coming home to see his baby. It was a good coincidence because it was also time to shave the baby, something traditionally done by the infant's grandmother. Musoda had been away for close to five months, during which time he maintained communication through letters. The letters took too long, but at least they arrived and he received replies. He had not specified his arrival date. He wanted to surprise them. He expected to find his wife frail as he had left her, not able to eat well due to pregnancy. His mother had fed her well. She had put on weight, and her childish face now looked grown. Her dimples were even deeper because of the now chubby cheeks.

When Musoda came home with two village children helping carry his bags, he looked different too. His calloused feet were hidden in shoes and socks. He wore long black trousers and a blue shirt. His hands were not as hard and calloused as they had been. He even wore some faint cologne. His hair was long, well-groomed and parted on one side of the head. When he saw his wife, he wanted to hug her but he didn't. It was considered "bad manners" to hug in public.

Kavosa was also too shy to look at him. They had to suppress their feelings until they were alone, as that's what was expected. This was a time for Musoda to hold Iminza, his firstborn daughter. They clicked at first sight. Musoda couldn't believe that Iminza was part of him and Kavosa.

Musoda dismissed the children who had helped him carry his bags by giving them one shilling each. He wanted to be alone with Kavosa and the baby, but no sooner had the children left did his mother come in, carrying tea and ripe bananas. Kadogo was also there after school, and her mother had to tell her that she didn't need to sleep in Kavosa's hut because Musoda was present. Kadogo didn't understand why it had to be so, but she obeyed. That's what children did. They obeyed all adults.

That night in the privacy of their hut, they caught up on what each one of them had missed. They were now comfortable because Musoda had brought a mattress and extra blankets, although the bed remained the same. They had to sleep tight because there was Iminza to be accommodated on the same bed, but parents always knew how to sleep with their babies in the same bed. A Maragoli woman, no matter how big her house is, cannot sleep far from her baby, like in some western countries where a baby sleeps in a different room, far from the parents.

At the age of five, the baby goes to sleep with the grandmother in rural settings. This may be different in urban settings, as people try to copy other cultures in the name of education.

That night, in each others' arms, they talked till the early morning hours, with Kavosa relating how her life had been for the whole year. She had become very good at working on the farm, planting, cultivating, and harvesting tomatoes, onions and cowpeas. They were just beginning to doze off in each other's arms when the cock crowed. Musoda had to get up early if he was going to accomplish the plans he had before traveled back to Kericho. He had learned the ways of town people and so he came out of his hut in boxer shorts only with a vest covering his upper body. He had a toothbrush with toothpaste on it. He started brushing his teeth as Kavosa handed him a cup of water to rinse his mouth.

He had asked for the water with toothpaste in his mouth, but the sound was muffled. She had to come closer to ask what he was saying. Moreover, Kavosa still brushed her teeth occasionally—like everyone else, with a twig that was chewed on one side to make it look like a tooth brush. Once in a period of close to a month there would be a thorough tooth cleaning, during which time one used a piece of charcoal or simply ashes, which made the teeth become whiter. Musoda was now beyond that because he lived in town.

The most important event of the day was the shaving of the baby's hair. It was mandatory for baby's first hair to be shaved with a razor and by the grandmother in the presence of both parents. It was done that morning before the sun rose in the sky. Important things were done in the morning because it was believed that more blessings came when the sun was still young. Musoda's mother sat down on the floor, where she had brought some water in a traditional basin made of clay. She held Iminza and washed her head before unwrapping a new razor from the package and shaved her clean. Iminza screamed as the sharp razor cleared her bush of curly, wooly hair. At one point there was a small cut at the back of the head. Kavosa held her stomach as she felt the pain her daughter was going though. The grandmothers said that the cut was a good sign that she would be a brave girl and that she was blessed. This may have been said to appease Kavosa, who obviously felt bad, but she would never argue with the elderly. It was taboo.

After the shaving, Musoda called his uncles and asked them to help him perform the act of paying dowry to Kavosa's parents. He had two cows, which had birthed calves. The villagers loved Kavosa because she brought good luck to the home. As soon as she had been there for about six months, both cows calved. She therefore had plenty of milk to drink when she gave birth to Iminza. Musoda was going to give one of the cows and its calf to Kavosa's parents in form of dowry. Those were counted as two cows. He also gave out two hundred shillings. Other women envied Kavosa because she had given her father two hundred shilling as a dowry, which was the most to be paid at the time. The total was to be three cows and two hundred shillings. One cow would be given later.

On the morning of the dowry, Musoda's uncle had to come to the home early to untie the cows. It wasn't supposed to be done by just anybody. The uncle handed the rope used to tether the cow to a young boy from their clan—a boy of about ten years in age. There were three other men who accompanied the boy to take the cows, with the uncle carrying the money. This served as an advance party, but a group of women would follow later, who had no particular job but to attend and eat. They found Kavosa's father and stepmother ready to welcome them.

The young boy drove the cows straight to the family's cowshed and tethered them. The cows had to urinate and pass dung in the shed before they could be brought outside to graze. Meanwhile, the three men and the boy were treated to tea and ground nuts while they waited for the group of women, including Kavosa. After they were done eating large pieces of chicken, it was time to go back. The young boy was paid ten shillings and a hen for the job he did.

The women came to carry some foodstuff like maize, flour, ready-made *ugali*, and a pot of chicken cooked whole. Only the insides had been removed. These things were not supposed to touch the ground until they reached their destination—in this case, Musoda's home. When they arrived back home, the uncle who untethered the cows was called once again to come and cut the whole chicken into pieces and give it to people to eat. It could not be done by anybody else, for that was the tradition.

With that done, Musoda felt accomplished. There was one thing he still had to do, but it had to wait. He was now used to living in slightly bigger houses in Kericho than his mud and grass-thatched hut. He wanted to put up a house for Kavosa—a house with a corrugated iron roof. There were plenty of trees that could be used as posts. The walls would be earthen, but the roof had to be different. The roof could also be used as a water catchment during rainy season, which would help Kavosa from her endless trips to the stream to fetch water. When he returned next time, he would bring some tanks for water storage.

This would be a task for his next visit because he had run out of cash, considering the work he had done plus handouts to villagers. He had to go back to work, save money, and come back. Unfortunately, if he were to save well, Kavosa would have to remain in the village a little longer. Kavosa loved and treated her husband too respectfully to argue. She had come to love Musoda's home like her own. She loved and respected Musoda's mother like her own as well. In her she found a mother she hadn't had since hers died.

There also was Grandma, who Kavosa found to have a vast knowledge about life. She always ran to her to ask questions as to how and why things would be done. One of the questions was why a baby has to have its first hair shaved by a grandmother. The answer was that it was a way of maintaining fidelity and purity of a clan. If, for example, a woman was adulterous, and had a baby outside her marriage, or if a girl had a baby without knowing who was responsible and tried to pin it to somebody else, there was a curse attached to the shaving from time immemorial. It was believed that if a baby was shaved by someone other than its blood grandmother, it would die instantly.

Everybody believed it happened but nobody was willing to try and disapprove it. Kavosa also learned that infidelity was a serious crime in Maragoli. If a woman had "walked outside," meaning if she had had an affair while married, she was not allowed to view her husband in the event of his death.

She would die instantly if she did. This put a lot of women in check. Kavosa therefore learned a lot from the grandmother.

The day Musoda left for Kericho, Kavosa had a heavy heart. She didn't want him to go, but again she thought it was for the betterment of their lives and felt better. She carried his bag that had his clothes and personal effects to Majengo from where he got transportation to Kericho. Kavosa walked back home, fighting back tears because grandma had told her that women didn't need to cry when their husbands traveled. It was a bad omen. Musoda also had earlier held his daughter Iminza for a long time, wishing he didn't have to go back to Kericho, but he consoled himself that things would get better.

So while Musoda was in Kericho, toiling and moiling with tea-picking in order to save money to improve their lives, Kavosa kept herself busy kneading clay for pottery, tending to Iminza, or leaving behind her daughter with Grandma or Kadogo as she carried pots to market.

Two weeks after Musoda went back to Kericho, Kavosa received a letter detailing how his journey was and that he had resumed work and was doing well. She immediately wrote back a reply. That is how life went for a whole year. Kavosa yearned for him even though she read letters from him from time to time. She wanted him—needed him actually. Sometimes she didn't believe that she had come to love this man who, together with his friends abducted he, carrying her shoulder high to his hut and caused her a lot of pain.

She thought the pain of being together with a man would always be there like that first time. She had come to get used to being with him and loved him very much. Musoda loved her too, and he remained the envy of other young men of his age in the village for having picked a very beautiful, humble, and loyal girl. He would find himself staring at her, especially when she talked. Her voice sounded musical to his ears. He loved her smile and loved to watch her dimpled cheeks. Life was good. He was now a father and husband, and needed to work hard to provide for his family. That's what men were supposed to do, and that's why it took him a year before he came home.

7

Musoda didn't announce his arrival home the second time. He just appeared at the time Kavosa was busy kneading clay while his mother was working on a water pot. Kavosa had since learned to make pots, but she had not yet acquired her mother-in-law's exquisite pottery skills. She made small ones for cooking the slimy *mutere*, vegetables, and others used to cook fish, which were round-mouthed with some ear-like projections on either side. Those were called *luyigira*. Musoda's mother was an expert in making the pots for making *ugali*, called *inyanguruga*, and the ones for cooking chicken, called *inyambeva*. No Maragoli woman lacked any of those pots in her house, and no woman could cook something else in a pot designed for another thing.

Kadogo, who was playing with Iminza, was the first to see Musoda. She shouted with excitement and ran to meet him, still holding the baby. This time there were about five people who helped carry his luggage. He had brought back corrugated iron roofing sheets, one large container for water storage, and a wooden bed. He had a suitcase in which he carried his clothes and those he had bought for Kavosa, Kadogo, and his mother. For Grandmother he brought a *leso* because she loved to cover herself with a wrapper over her dress when she went anywhere. There was a carton box in which he had put some foodstuff like bread, rice and cooking oil, not forgetting oil for making *chapati*.

Kavosa washed her hands quickly and went to welcome him shyly. She made some tea and set it on the small table he had made for her. Musoda ordered her to open the box with bread so they could eat some. She called Mama and grandma to come and have some tea with the visitor. Kadogo was meanwhile running after a loudly squawking chicken. The chicken ran to the house for dear life, and Kadogo closed the door and pounced on it. Gasping for air, she handed it to Kavosa, who thanked her and asked her to sit down and have some tea. Kavosa tethered the chicken for a while so it couldn't escape as she fed Iminza with bread before going to her mother-in-law's house to slaughter and prepare the chicken for supper.

After taking tea, Musoda played with Iminza for a while, although she didn't really know him. She rejected him at first but warmed up quickly when she saw everybody happy with him. Then he embarked on assembling the pieces of wood he called a bed into one. It was wide and nearly took up all the space in the house. He had brought a wide enough mattress to go with it. That night they were more comfortable than they had ever been!

There wasn't much sleeping that night though. They cuddled and talked till the early hours of morning. Kavosa related how she had spent her whole year while he was away. Apart from making pots with her mother-in-law, she had mastered the art of working on the farm: planting, cultivating and harvesting tomatoes, onions, and cowpeas for sale. She loved taking wares to the market to bring home some money for subsistence. That way, they lessened the burden on Musoda's wages.

Though still at a tender age of eighteen, she had become a very responsible woman. Musoda explained how the tea was picked—that the faster one was, the more one earned. They were paid by the weight they picked. Musoda had become one of the best and fastest tea-pickers, and even his supervisor liked him and forwarded his name for a bonus. That's how he came to afford all the things he had brought. Iminza was peacefully sleeping on the floor on the year-old mattress, oblivious to the talk of her parents.

Kadogo's father, who was Musoda's clan uncle, the man who inherited Musoda's mother, arrived at Musoda's house very early the following morning. Musoda was already awake and work had to begin. The man hand-picked to do the construction of the semi-permanent house was already there. Boys from the village had been called to cut down trees and turn them into posts. Some were there to dig up holes in which to put poles. They all gathered at a spot where the house could be erected. Musoda's uncle said a prayer and put a peg in the ground where the center of the house would be. A nice rectangle was formed with pegs in the four corners. A rope was tied around the rectangle with smaller pegs along the sides. The inside of the rectangle was also marked for one main bedroom, one spare bedroom, a living room, and a kitchen. The kitchen would only be a place for kitchen utensils. Musoda's old hut would be the kitchen. Nobody wanted to spoil a good house with smoke, so the house was planted right in front of the hut.

The compound was as busy as a beehive. Some people were digging holes while others were fixing the posts and others were bringing in long poles for beams. By the end of the day, the whole structure was set. The following day would be for roofing and some men would be making mud for the walls. Village women, in the true spirit of African socialism, had come to offer their help with ferrying in water for making mud. They would also help put the mud in place to make the walls of the house. They didn't expect payment of any kind.

The third day was set aside to cover the top of the house. Musoda's uncle once again came to hand the last iron sheet to the *fundi,* and then proceeded to slaughter the rooster that had been covered under a basket for the occasion. The *fundi* was also a local carpenter who made wooden doors and windows. As soon as he saw Musoda bring in iron sheets, he went ahead making doors and windows, hoping they would be purchased. Indeed, they served a purpose. There were two main doors for the front and back and four lighter ones for the inside. Musoda also bought the five wooden windows needed. Within a week, the house was ready for occupation thanks to the Maragoli social skills. The villagers had wholeheartedly helped Musoda make a house. The remaining part of smoothening the walls and whitewashing them with white clay was to be done gradually by Kavosa herself, with the help of her village friends. She had longed for a house she could decorate like other women, and now God had heard her prayer. She was going to make it stand out in the village. She didn't even entertain the idea of going to Kericho like her friends had done. She loved it in the village as long as Musoda kept writing her letters.

A week after occupying the new house, it was time for Kavosa to start "cooking," which meant that she was to be given official mandate to start cooking her own food in her house. Her mother-in-law had molded and baked the three stones that made a hearth. She brought them and laid them strategically in the new kitchen. On that day the clan had been summoned to come and witness it.

Kadodo, her sister-in-law, would make a fire, place a pot over it, and pour in some water. Before that, Kavosa had gone back to her father's home to get some flour for the occasion as required by tradition. She also invited her stepmother to the occasion but she declined because she didn't particularly like Kavosa. Now, when the water in the pot for *ugali* started boiling, Kadogo invited Kavosa to come and make the ugali. She handed her the cooking stick and stepped aside for Kavosa to do the remaining work. Kavosa made the ugali and dished it out to all the guests and villagers who had come to witness the ceremony. They were all satisfied that she was a good cook and could be "given her pot" as it was said.

Kavosa started cooking food in what used to be her hut but was now her kitchen. She averted the fears of her mother-in-law that she would have to cook on her own again, by telling her that they were only four people in the family plus Iminza who was still a toddler. There was no need for each of them to prepare their own food. She offered to be the main cook, and they would all converge in her house for meals. Kadogo's father visited occasionally but lived with his main wife a mile away. It didn't matter that he had a wife and children when he was assigned to inherit Musoda's mother. Tradition demanded it, and no woman would stand in the way of elders. Not even Musoda's mother could reject anybody given to her.

A week after the cooking ceremony, it was time for Musoda to go back to Kericho. He had stayed for a total of four weeks during his leave days. He was happy with the work he had done. His wife had a nice house, and being the only surviving son, he had the burden of constructing his mother's house next time he came. Clan elders had prevailed upon him to build his mother's house before building his own but he rejected the idea, saying he didn't want his daughter to catch pneumonia in the hut that was dripping water all over during rainy season. Some tried to threaten him, saying it was taboo to "cover your head"—meaning having a good roof over your head—before your parents, but he wouldn't hear any of it. He reasoned that his family came first, and that when he came back home for leave after one year, his main objective would be to construct his mother's house.

Some elders went home complaining that "the child of Asengi" who was so humble and respectful had changed because of the ways of town.

"It must be that girl that is giving him such a big head!" Ngereso, one of the elders that had tried to advise him, said, poking the ground with his walking stick for emphasis.

"The world is changing," said his friend Kayugira, shrugging his shoulders. "Young people cannot be doing things the way we did them . . ."

"If this world were left to the youth, they would ruin it completely!" Ngereso whined before spitting to express his disgust. To him "the world" did not extend beyond their village.

Musoda's mother didn't even care. She knew her son meant well. He had married a good woman who was respectful and hardworking. He had left the village to go to greener pastures so he could support her and his family. "What is a house? Do I live outside?" she wondered. She knew her son and knew he would do as he promised.

Musoda prepared to leave home for Kericho on a Sunday morning. His mother came to his house in the morning to pray for him. Kavosa, as usual, carried his bag of clothes to Majengo. He normally took a bus to Kisumu to connect with another bus that went to Kericho. That morning, he was lucky to have found a bus that belonged to a company called Bus Union that plied the Kaimosi-Nairobi route. This meant that he wouldn't have to take two bus rides to Kericho like he normally would.

The bus was already at the bus stop, and the agents were frantically fighting for passengers to fill their buses. Musoda decided to take the bus because, after all, there was no other route to Nairobi but via Kericho. He boarded it after saying farewell to Kavosa and found himself a window seat from which he could see Kavosa as she walked back home. Kavosa was not in a hurry to go. She just stood there, looking at him and talking to him through the window. She had been taught by some people that when she took somebody to board a bus or any vehicle, she should make a point of remembering the registration of the vehicle. She noted that this orange colored bus was registered as vehicle number KNB 666. When the bus started moving, Kavosa fought a tear but couldn't contain it. Tears rolled down her face as she wiped them with a piece of cloth she carried to serve as a handkerchief. She cried all the way home, grateful she didn't meet anybody she knew, who would have wanted to know if she was alright.

As she neared her house, she stopped crying. She went to the house and found Kadogo holding Iminza, who was dozing off. She took her and breastfed her until she fully went to sleep. Kavosa was very unsettled. She was bored. She wished it wasn't a Sunday so she could go to work on the farm. Christians and all in the village knew that Sunday was a resting day. Besides cooking and eating, nobody worked on a Sunday. Her mind was racing, and she didn't know what it was. These feelings were on and off for a whole week while Kavosa hoped that she would receive a letter from Musoda. Letters took at least two weeks to arrive, and so it was nerve-wracking.

The following Sunday, Musoda's friend from Kericho came home bearing some puzzling news. Immediately upon arrival, he went over to Musoda's home to ask why his friend had not reported to work in Kericho yet. His supervisor needed him to go back right away.

It was all so worrying! Musoda had left a week earlier for Kericho. Where did he go? Did the bus just pass Kericho without stopping and take him to Nairobi? Those were the questions people asked each other.

Soon, a search group had been organized. Kavosa prayed that her husband would be alright. She told the search party that she remembered the registration number of the bus as KNB 666, and the company of the bus was Bus Union. At least now the party had something to start with. A group of six men went to Majengo to ask if anybody had seen the bus with the name and registration as indicated.

At Majengo, Kavosa confronted some horrible news. One of the agents told them that the bus had been involved in a road accident at Nyamasaria after it left Kisumu and before it reached Ahero. Some of the searchers had to go to

Kisumu because they didn't have enough money to carry everybody to Kisumu.

On arrival at Kisumu police station, their worst fears were confirmed. They were told about an accident in Nyamasaria. One kind policeman explained to them that the described bus had a tire burst in the middle of the road. The driver had managed to maneuver the bus to the side of the road. Mechanics were called, and as they were trying to repair the tire, the passengers were told to come out of the bus to make it easier to work the power jack.

Some of the more tired ones continued sitting next to the bus outside, watching frantic mechanics trying to work the repairs. Suddenly, a truck had come from the opposite side, speeding and with full lights on.

To avoid hitting an oncoming car head-on, the truck driver had swerved to the left of the bus, ploughing into everybody that was standing there, including the mechanics. Several people died on the spot while others were admitted at New Nyanza General Hospital and Ahero and Nyamasaria Dispensaries. On hearing this, the search party started with the Dispensaries and both private and government hospitals. They were all in a state of denial, refusing to believe that Musoda would be among those who died. Failing to find him in hospitals, they went home to inform the relatives the news they had heard. Kavosa refused to eat and tied a strip of banana fiber around her waist. So many people came to converge at the home to comfort Kavosa and her mother-in-law. Grandmother prayed that she would be the one to die before her grandson. Musoda's mother was hopeful that he would be found alive. Since nobody was cooking in the home, neighbors brought in cooked meals to support the family. Some offered to care for Iminza while her mother was distraught.

In the morning, the search party converged again at the home. Musoda's uncle had sold a cow for a pittance just to get money for the search party to spend while they searched for Musoda. They left in the morning after a prayer by the uncle. In Kisumu they were apprehensive about going to the mortuaries. There used to be stories that all the dead were heaped together in a room, and one had to dig through the bodies to find one's relative. It was even worse when people speculated that a qualified doctor had to pass one more test in order to be registered as one, and that was to sleep in the mortuary alone with the dead. According to the stories, many would-be doctors quit the profession at this point.

But this was Musoda they were searching for—their friend, their cousin . . . a son, father, and husband. They had to find him come sunshine or rain. They searched Ahero, Nyamasaria, and Kisumu's hospitals in vain. They now had to go to the only mortuary around the area, and that was in Kisumu.

They approached the mortuary fretfully. There was an attendant who talked to them nicely, asking what they wanted. They described Musoda's appearance, and the attendant told them that all the dead had been identified . . . except for three bodies that were involved in the Nyamasaria accident. The bodies were to be disposed of tomorrow if nobody claimed them. "We only keep unknown bodies for ten days, and today is the tenth day, meaning tomorrow morning those three bodies would be buried in one common grave," he explained.

It is taboo for a Maragoli to be buried anywhere other than his home. Their bodies have to be transported back to their ancestral land for burial. It was disheartening to hear that if Musoda was dead and not found, wherever the body was, it would be buried the next day. Two of the searchers felt brave enough to follow the attendant into the mortuary to check on those three bodies.

One body resembled that of Musoda but he had been crashed badly, and his teeth had been hit out of the mouth. Moreover, the body was so much swollen that it did not look like Musoda. Those who knew his legs and set of toes almost confirmed that it was Musoda. The two men called in the rest of the search party, who observed the body but didn't know what to make of it. One of them suggested going back home to get Musoda's mother and Kavosa.

When Kavosa and her mother-in-law arrived, it didn't take them long to identify the body. Musoda's mother said that his son had a birthmark under his right arm. If they could see it, then he was the one. For sure, when they tried to lift his right hand, stiff as it was. The mother addressed his body as if he could actually hear her "Musoda, if this is you let us lift your right arm and see your birthmark." Implausibly, the arm became flexible, and there was the birthmark, a dark round spot under his arm. Kavosa identified his finger, which was still in a band aid after a stick had pierced his skin while he was working on the house. She also recognized the green boxer shorts he'd been wearing on the day he left home.

Words travel faster than lighting. In no time, the whole village knew that Musoda had died in a road accident on his way back to Kericho. Everyone in the village wailed and mourned. His mother was lost for words. She fainted several times, and every time people applied first aid the only way they knew. Women surrounded her, fanning her with their *lesos*. They sent for a soda and tried to make her drink as it ran down her cheeks. She would come to for a while, then pass out again. But on her way home from identifying Musoda, Kavosa didn't utter a word. She was quiet. Some people started pointing fingers at her, asking why she wasn't crying. Some even went as far as accusing her of having been the cause of his untimely death.

In the village, she grabbed Iminza so tight that people thought she would choke the life out of her. Femina, the woman who helped her deliver the baby was also an expert in consoling the bereaved. She held her hand quietly and took her to her bedroom. She started provoking her to cry. "Your husband is gone. The one you used to share this bed with. From now on, you will be alone. He will never come back. You will be both mother and father to Iminza. Everybody you see crying outside will go to their homes and be happy but you will be alone," she said.

Those words pierced Kavosa like a knife to the heart. She burst out crying loudly and hysterically. Femina had achieved the desired effect. She just wanted Kavosa to cry her shock out. She wanted her to release the pressure and not bottle it up inside her. Femina had just helped Kavosa turn on the tear tap. She cried uncontrollably. She sang dirges. She narrated the plans they had together. She said Musoda had replaced her mother, who had successfully turned into pleasant memories, for beside her mother, Musoda was the only one who truly loved her. He was now gone, and Kavosa was back to square one. Back to having a whole house to herself, like when her mother died, and she had to live all alone.

When people saw Kavosa running out of the house wailing, they all wailed with her. Femina had succeeded in taking Iminza from her. The whole village was in a somber mood. It was a sad time for the villagers of Masizi village.

The crying and wailing went on for about three hours, and then the clan elders got together to sit and discuss the burial. Musoda, like his father, had died a *kirumindo* death, unnatural and before his time. This was a category of death for those who died from accidents, homicides, suicides, and drowning. Following such deaths, people cried for a while but had to remain silent during the burial.

The clan elders discussed how to get transportation of the body from Kisumu. There was a certain teacher in the neighboring village of Gavalagi who owned a pickup truck. He offered to ferry the body home. Relieved, the clan elders thanked him and made arrangements for the gravedigging in the middle of the night. The body had to be buried immediately upon arriving home.

Musoda's uncle went into his mother's house and brought out hoes, spades, and machetes for the digging of the grave. According to tradition, the grave-digging could only be done by the one whom Musoda called "father" or "uncle." The uncle also got instructions as to how the bonfire would be started. Most of the villagers would spend the night in this home, singing or wailing. Some women came to sleep in any space in the houses. While the grave was being dug, one clan elder would be assigned the work of slaughtering the cockerel meant to be consumed by the gravediggers upon completion of their task. Everything was done by the old man, all the way down to boiling water with which to remove the cockerel's feathers.

Those going to Kisumu to get the body left home at four o'clock in the morning. Arrangements had been made with the night mortuary attendant to release the body early enough. Mortuaries fees were not needed at that time, so they only gave the attendant a small tip for him to get a cup of tea. The body was back home by seven o'clock. Clan elders signaled mourners to remain quiet. You could have heard a pin drop. Not even Kavosa or Iminza were allowed to make any sound.

As soon as the vehicle stopped, the men grabbed the body and headed straight to the grave. The uncle went into the house and emerged with a one-month-old chick. He handed it to the owner of the pickup truck. He immediately left the home and drove off. As he headed home, he threw the chick out through the window and let it go. This was meant to release any bad omen that had followed him by carrying the dead to fly away with the chick. He did not go home straight but went to a river to clean his truck.

Using milk from a gourd, an old man blessed the body by drinking the milk and spraying it on the body, uttering things like, "Your time to go had not been reached. Somebody has caused you your life. Follow and torment them. But do not come back to disturb the people in this home."

The body was then lowered into the grave, with no service or prayer. The people who dug the grave were again ready to cover it up. They knew there was another cockerel. With such a death, the grave is not left with a heap of red earth. It was spread level. It was after the leveling of the grave that people were allowed to talk and move around. Those who still wanted to mourn could now do so. Kavosa was brought a stool to sit next to the grave for hours on end. The stool was stationed at the head. This was to prove that Kavosa had not known any other man apart from her husband. In fact, some women had talked to her about it before the body was brought home. Those who had committed adultery would not view the bodies of their husbands lest they die on the spot. After the burial, the stool would be put at the feet.

Because young children were not allowed to witness this kind of burial, they were made to stay in the banana plantations behind the houses. As for Kavosa, the villagers had to prove that she had not gone astray and slept with another man. They took Musoda's shirt and jacket and had her wear them. As if that wasn't enough, she had to put on his hat and hold his walking stick all the time she was mourning. It was widely believed that she would have dropped dead if she had had another man while married to Musoda. Nothing happened because she had been faithful to her husband, although she found it ridiculous that she was meant to go through that intimidation just to prove her innocence. She had to remain dressed in that manner, without taking a bath for three days after the burial.

After three days, the clan assembled for the resurrection rites and the ceremonial shaving of hair. Everybody in the home had their hair shaved clean. The first to be shaved had to be a young boy in the home. Since there were no male children in Musoda's home, the first to be shaved was a grandson of his uncle. Even Iminza was shaved on that day. Only Kavosa was going to be shaved the following day.

The following morning, this was done by a widow from the clan, as was required. She shaved Kavosa's head clean.

Moreover, she shaved her eyebrows and her pubic hair too. Every hair on the body of the widow or widower had to be shaved off. Kavosa was a pathetic sight, shaven clean of her hair and eyebrows. The same widow who shaved her was responsible for making her meals and preparing her baths.

Kavosa wasn't supposed to sit and eat with other people until her hair grew back. In fact, she had to attend the call of nature on the grass, and the widow assigned to her would check to see if the grass where she peed was dry. It was believed that stress made some widow's urine become acidic, and that would be bad for the widow and the children who associated with her before her hair grew. It was believed that their bodies would ripen like bananas and they would die. It was therefore better to avoid such catastrophes.

The same widow who shaved Kavosa performed other rituals. It was mandatory that somebody other than the people in the homestead sweep all the houses clean. Nobody swept the houses while they were still in mourning. The widow had to sweep and scoop all the ashes from the hearths. After this, people could return to living normally, but she stayed with Kavosa for two weeks. On her departure, she was given a chicken and some flour in gratitude for her good work.

8

A month after the death of Musoda, another gathering was held which marked the last of the mourning process. This was the *lovego* feast. Kavosa had not even come to terms with the absence of her husband in the home. Somehow, in her mind he was in Kericho, and he would eventually come home. She still cried herself to sleep. *Lovego* was for the clan to sit and feast on a bull if the departed had been a man and a cow if it had been a woman. *Lovego* was only observed once for people who were married and had children. Musoda had Kavosa and Iminza, and so he qualified.

Clan elders picked a day for the celebration. They sent two men to go to the market and buy a bull for the purpose. The men had to be very careful in choosing the bull. It had to have all body parts intact. They observed even the tail to make sure it wasn't crooked. They also made sure that it hadn't been sterilized or castrated. Having found one, they bargained and paid the price, then walked the bull all the way on foot from Luanda market.

The home was abuzz with activity on the day of remembrance. The bull was to be slaughtered at dawn. Clan members and villagers alike converged at the home to beg for pieces of meat to take home. The remaining meat was cooked in the home for the feast. But first there was a meeting in which an elder who acted as the clan's chairman led the clan in asking those who had Musoda's debts to say so. Those who Musoda owed anything also made their case. After the discussion and the debtor agreed to pay the debt, the chairman asked the crowd if it agreed. The crowd agreed in unison, and the chairman would hit the table in the same way judges use their gavels at he conclusion of a case. Actually, a case settled at a *lovego* was admissible in a court of law as evidence, if the debtor refused to pay.

After the debts discussion and conclusion, the chairman announced that there was one more important subject they had to deal with before they ate. The subject had something to do with Kavosa's inheritance.

"This girl has our child, and she is a good girl. We cannot let her go, and she can't live alone forever. We need to find somebody to shoulder the late Musoda's responsibility," he concluded as the other clan members agreed with him, applauding and nodding their heads.

Kavosa sat quietly with other women on the ground, at a place assigned to women. During remembrances, women weren't supposed to stand to address the meeting. They answered questions while seated on the ground if and when asked. It was mainly an affair for men. Only they could stand and speak to the elders.

Kavosa was worried, wondering whom she would be given to. She could see young men in the crowd throwing glances at her, and she wondered if it would be one of them.

One man suggested a name to which other men objected, saying the suggested man was older than Musoda by a few years. It had to be someone younger than Musoda. The reason was that an older brother or cousin would act as a father in the absence of the head of the home. Another man was suggested, but an old clan elder calculated when he was circumcised and said no. "For one, he is like an uncle to Musoda, and another, he was circumcised in an earlier group than Musoda. We need a young man almost the age of Musoda and a close relative, like a cousin. The only person I see fit for this job is Sozi."

Sozi was a distant cousin of Musoda's who used to work with him. If Musoda had a tree to cut down and hewn for somebody, he would ask Sozi to help, and they would split the wages. He was a generally decent young man, but he drank the local alcoholic brew called *busaa* and the other known as *chang'aa*. Most in the gathering were in agreement on Sozi, and the clan elders also agreed to ask Sozi to stop drinking and smoking cannabis.

Kavosa listened quietly and felt her stomach revolting like she was getting sick. She stood up and went behind the house to throw up. She hadn't been eating very well since the death of her husband. Now her mind was racing. She loved Musoda very much. He was barely cold in his grave, yet the old men were giving her another husband even before she has time to fully mourn her husband. It was incomprehensible.

The crowd misunderstood Kavosa's action as being rude to the clan elders. They sent a woman to go call her, explaining that she should be careful never to leave such a meeting when important matters are being discussed. They said it was all to her benefit. The woman found Kavosa puking and shaking uncontrollably. She beckoned Kavosa's mother-in-law, who came immediately. Both women concluded that Kavosa was now vomiting shock out of her system.

They led her to the house and lay her on her bed. They placed a piece of broken pot near the bed to serve as a basin in case she felt like puking. Femina was called in because apart from being a traditional birth attendant, she knew about herbs that could cure other ailments like malaria, stomachache, earache, and general fatigue. Femina immediately went to work. She started by taking Kavosa's temperature on her brow using the back of her hand, then felt her chest, and finally asked her to lie on her back as she lifted her clothes up. Femina washed her hands and applied soap so she could massage Kavosa's belly. She massaged the belly with so much concentration it was as if she was reading the sonogram in her mind. Finally, she asked Kavosa if she was pregnant. Kavosa was startled and seemed to be only aware of her condition. She remembered that her last period was a week before Musoda came home, and he stayed for a whole month. It has been one month since he died. That would mean she was two months pregnant.

This was going through her head, but she chose to answer Femina's question with, "I don't know."

Femina kept pressing, asking when she had her last period, to which she answered, "Two months ago. It was over a week before Musoda came home."

The women got excited. They couldn't think otherwise because Kavosa hadn't left home since her husband's death, and relatives still kept her company in her house until *lovego* was over.

Kavosa's mother-in-law, at the command of Femina went to tell the elders to stop the discussion because they had just discovered that Kavosa was "heavy"—a word politely used in Maragoli circles instead of pregnant. According to Maragoli customs, any discussion about dowry or inheritance would be shelved whenever the woman in question was pregnant, until the baby was born. And after the baby was born, Kavosa would be taken care of to recuperate for at least three months before the clan elders would assemble to officially bless the union between Kavosa and Sozi.

As happy as Sozi was for being chosen among many to inherit Musoda's widow who was beautiful and respectful, he couldn't take matters in his hands. He had to respect the elders. He had to wait until the baby was born and the elders converged once again to officially hand him to her. For the time being, he would pass by, see if she needed anything, but never stay too long. Kavosa knew the tradition and was glad that she was pregnant, which would give her time to observe and weigh if she could trust Sozi to take Musoda's place. In the back of her mind she doubted it. She loved Musoda too much—even in death. He was her first and only one. The gap he left in her heart would be hard to fill even by his close friend and relative, Sozi.

Sozi had been married before, but they had parted ways with his wife because of his drinking habits. He would come home drunk and start beating his wife for no reason. When the wife had had enough of it, she left and never turned back. She was now happily married to a widower in Bunyore. In those times, a woman who was once married would only remarry a widower. These kind of women were called "chain cutters," and few in their right mind would marry such a woman.

Therefore, it was the clan's prayer that giving Sozi to Kavosa would help him settle down. The clan wasn't happy to have an unmarried adult in their village. No one considered the fact that Kavosa had her own feelings and opinion—that she may not exactly like the idea of being inherited by the village drunk. She was the clan's property, and they could make any decisions on her behalf. Women were supposed to take it as it was handed down to them, no questions asked, or else it would be construed to mean disrespect.

It would also have mattered little if Sozi's wife was still there. Maragolis were well known for their polygamy. Women were supposed to accept another wife without questions. Arguing and making a scene would be taken as jealousy, and nobody wanted to be called jealous or envious in the community.

Kavosa continued to help with the pot-making and the farming, while raising her daughter Iminza on her own. Sozi would come around, play with Iminza for a while, get *liise* grass from downstream to repair the thatched kitchen when it leaked, and perform other menial jobs in the home.

Kavosa would cook and set a plate before him, which Sozi devoured, grunting between mouthfuls that the food was so delicious. He would always walk back to his hut, never forcing anything but patiently waiting for the clan elders to decide. That would be three months after the birth of the coming baby. Every so often, Sozi would count on his fingers and announce to nobody in particular six months to go, four months to go, and then it was only three months to go!

9

Like during the first pregnancy, Kavosa was awakened by a sharp pain on her lower back. She tried to stretch herself back but instead got a felt a muscle pull in one of her legs. She moaned in agony, waking Kadogo who still kept her company in the big house. To her it was a matter of prestige to have a room of her own—of course apart from the company she provided for Kavosa and Iminza, who mainly shared a bed with her mother but sometimes staggered to Kadogo's room. They had come to bond and love each other immensely. Iminza had for the most part forgotten about her daddy, thanks to the death that took him too early.

This was one of the nights Iminza had clung to Kadogo like she knew what was coming. Before Kavosa explained to Kadogo what was happening, there was another pain across her abdomen. As she writhed in pain, Kadogo suspected what was going on. She quickly opened the door and ran to call her mother. Her mother woke up and went to get Femina, the village midwife. It was time for another baby.

This time round, Kavosa knew what to expect, and she knew the rules. The labor was also shorter than last time. It was at three o'clock in the morning when she felt the first contraction, and by eight o'clock in the morning she had her baby. Everybody prayed for a boy so he could be given Musoda's name, as was traditionally done. Babies born in a clan were mostly given the name of the most recently deceased, depending on the gender. As Femina pulled on the baby, urging Kavosa to push, the baby dropped out with a scream. It was another girl! Kavosa was grateful for two things: that the ordeal was over and that God had given her a girl so she could name her after her mother. It was therefore disheartening to read disappointment on everybody's faces. Musoda's mother even blurted out, "It's another frog," a derogatory term people would give to baby girls due to their unshapely appearance at birth.

Having a baby boy would have strengthened Kavosa's standing in the community. She would have been respected more. But now they didn't see her beauty and respect anymore. All they saw was a widow who couldn't give her husband a replacement. Things started changing. Nobody was willing to take care of Kavosa for the three months after the baby was born. She wished Musoda was alive. Musoda's mother even refused to name the baby after herself. Only Kadogo would come from school and try to do everything for her. As a result, Kavosa had to start working before the three months were up and suffered frequent backaches as a result.

Kavosa was accused of everything in Masizi Village just because she didn't get a boy as expected. The death of her husband was revisited and blamed on her. Her mother-in-law insisted that Musoda died because he had refused to listen to the elders and build a house for his mother before building his own. She even blamed Kavosa for forcing him to do it. "Musoda had been a good boy until this woman came into his life," she complained. Some villagers even started discouraging Sozi to stay away from "that woman" or else he would die like Musoda.

Kavosa's mother-in-law even barred Kadogo from sleeping in her house. Two weeks before the stipulated three months, Kavosa woke up at five o'clock in the morning. She hadn't even wash her face. She had tied her few belongings in a *leso* the previous night. She took the sleepy Iminza and strapped her to her back. She put the bundle of her belongings on her head and scooped up Afandi, the baby, in her arms and stepped out into the cool morning air. She felt her way with her bare feet as she walked away into the unknown. There was only one place she could have gone. Her mother's house was still intact.

One of her stepbrothers, the only reasonable one, lived in the house with his two-year-old son. The son was in dire need of care. He had jiggers all over his body. Her stepbrother had gotten a girl pregnant in the village, but the girl's parents refused to let him marry her. They instead chose to marry her off to an old man from Tarime, who had given them many cows. The baby was therefore dumped at the house, but his mother refused to take care of it. When Kavosa came back to the house, arriving at eight o'clock in the morning with tears in her eyes, the first thing she did was clean the house, then clean her brother's son. Everyone in Gaago village learned that Kavosa was back and sympathized with the treatment those Masizi village people had accorded her. Those who maintained that a woman's purpose in society was to get married consoled her, saying not to worry, as she would get another husband.

After Kavosa came back home, her stepbrother couldn't live in the same house with her. He had to seek accommodation with other people until he was able to put up his own hut. Kavosa took over the care of his son like he was her own. She now had three children to feed.

Meanwhile, back in Masizi village, Kadogo, who loved Iminza very much, though having been pulled from Kavosa's house by her mother, made a point of going to that house every morning to see Iminza before proceeding to school. Kadogo touched the door on that morning and it clicked open. She called out "Iminza, Iminza." Upon hearing no reply, she called out "Mulamwa!" (sister-in-law) but there was no answer.

She entered the house and checked every room, but there was no sound. She went to Kavosa's bedroom and found the bed empty. That's when she noticed that the mattress was on the bed but there were no blankets and no children around. She said to no one in particular, "She's gone," as she ran out of the house to go tell her mother. Her mother wasn't really concerned that Kavosa was gone. The first thing she asked for was the mattress. She had been craving the mattress ever since Musoda brought it home. Moreover, the fact that Kavosa was gone meant that she could now move into her house and live comfortably.

Kadogo cried, already missing her sister-in-law and her niece, Iminza, and the baby, Afandi. Her mother yelled at her to stop crying. That's when the neighbors heard about it and came to converge at the home.

Some neighbors felt that Kavosa was treated badly since her husband died. But Kavosa was gone. Someone in the crowd suggested that they go and check at her father's home to see if that was where she'd gone. Another one quipped,

"No! You will all be beaten. Avaguuga are not to be played with. We must admit that we treated their daughter badly."

In the long run, they agreed to have someone spy secretly. That person would be Sozi because he had developed a liking for Kavosa. That evening, Sozi went back to report to the village that he saw Kavosa, with a baby strapped on her back, carrying a pot of water from the stream. "Then we must demand our cows we gave them in dowry back" said one clan elder. "Not when she has given us two children," answered another elder. "Those children belong here. She will raise them but we will get cows from them because children always belong to the father's clan" he concluded.

Musoda's mother had already moved into Kavosa's house. Some villagers then started calling her a witch. "She is the one who wanted her son to die so she could inherit the house," said one neighbor. Many others agreed that she had handled her daughter-in-law wrongly since her son died.

Back home in Gaago, the villagers were quite receptive. They welcomed Kavosa, they empathized with her, and they consoled her. They were sorry that she had lost her husband but assured her that a man of her type would come around and marry her. Their main concern was that a woman must be married. Most of the women brought her cooked food, and others gave her maize and sorghum. Some offered her garden vegetables, telling her to go pluck whenever she felt like. She always thanked them politely. Kavosa felt at home. In Masizi village, she was like an ugly duckling among chickens since her husband died, but now she felt like a duck among other ducks.

Kavosa joined women in Gaago village to till their fields. She joined their merry-go-round support groups in which they contributed money to assist each other in turns—hence the name. Kavosa bought a bed and a mattress with her merry-go-round money. Since she came back, she had been sleeping on the floor on a papyrus mat, which she had forgotten all about after three years while married.

After only six month's stay back home, Kavosa had returned to her normal self. She was happy and one could now notice her dimples again. The frown she had been wearing since the death of her husband had been erased. She felt she had to be happy for the sake of her children and her nephew, who now called her "Mama" as well.

The boy, Ajega, was the same age as Iminza, and had a resemblance since they were cousins. This made people think that they were twins, and Kavosa allowed them to think so because she had come to love Ajega like her own son. By this time, her brother, Ajega's father, had just disappeared into thin air. He abdicated his parenthood to his half-sister, Kavosa, and seemed to not care about the boy anymore. Some people speculated that he had gone to Nyahera to live with a Luo widow, while others said he was in Kericho. But another group even suggested he was dead.

Perhaps the only speculation that was closest to the truth was that he had been seen in Mombasa and had changed his name to an Islamic one. This proved to be somewhat true because because after several years, he visited the village dressed in a *kanzu* like a Muslim and never talked about his son.

Kavosa didn't care because she would never have parted with Ajega. She wanted to give her children the life she never had. She wanted them to go to school and be important people and even buy cars. That was her biggest aim.

10

Kavosa was determined to make sure that her three children got an education. She had to find ways and means of getting money to pay tuition. Few people were going to help her. Her father was old, and by then her brother had migrated to Kitale and hardly ever came home. Moreover, the burden would be too great for somebody who had his own problems. She would have to think hard. Then an idea struck her. With her next merry-go-round money she would start a small business. She would buy fruits and vegetables and sell them in Kisumu and Eldoret.

The business started slowly, but after four months, everybody seemed to know her. She knew how to handle her customers, always smiling.

When the business and the care of children became overwhelming, she took in a clan cousin, Mideva, who had been sent away from several marriages because she couldn't bear children. She desperately needed a place to stay, as her brothers didn't allow her to live in the home. They always reminded her that a woman's place was with her husband and not her brothers. Kavosa saw her as a God-send because then she could leave children in her care as she went from market to market.

Mideva was several years older than Kavosa. Mideva was short and a bit plump, and like Kavosa, she was beautiful with one dimple on her left cheek. She must have been a knockout in her youthful days if her beauty was still visible even after going through hell on earth. Her first husband loved her very much, but after being together for seven years without a child, her mother-in-law sent her packing. She lived with her mother, who lived for another three years.

Her second husband came along and they went to live in Mombasa. For three years she tried to conceive in vain. She went from doctor to doctor but couldn't get pregnant. The man wanted a baby, so he married somebody else and threw Mideva out of the house.

Her third husband was very abusive. She left him after five years. The fourth and last husband she had was a nice man and tried to tolerate her infertility, but her in-laws were impatient with her. She was called all the mean names in the dictionary, and some people went as far as telling her that she was in their home just to fill up their pit latrines, meaning she was too shitty to be acceptable in the family without any benefits. She was hurt to the core.

Unlike Kavosa, Mideva's mother's house had been demolished after her death, her father having died years earlier. Her brothers didn't allow her to live in their houses. She was elated to find Kavosa living in the same village, in her mother's house and tilling her mother's garden.

She approached Kavosa with fear, thinking she would be offended if she asked to move in with her. "Can you please allow me get accommodation in your house for a few days before I figure out my next move?" she asked. Kavosa answered her without hesitation, saying that she wouldn't care if she chose to live with her forever. Mideva was so happy that she got her few belongings and came to stay with Kavosa. Thus she became a sort of live-in maid, taking care of the children while Kavosa was busy with her small business.

For a while, the two women, whose lives had started off on a painful note, became happy. Mideva took great care of the children, whom she immensely loved like her own. Kavosa was happy to have gotten a helper in her cousin. At least now she could concentrate on the business. When she came home, the children were well fed and happy. There was always well-prepared food kept for her. In appreciation for what Mideva did for her, she bought her clothes similar to hers, and also gave her some pocket money for anything she needed.

With the home situation taken care off, Kavosa embarked on looking for bigger markets for her wares. She dealt in fruits and vegetables. The main fruits she sold were paw paws, avocados, guavas, mangos, and passion fruit. The vegetables included cabbage, kale, collard greens, and some indigenous African vegetable like *mito, mutere, zisaaga, livogoi,* and *lisuuza.* She kept observing and listening to whatever customers needed and would bring it next time. Sometimes, Mideva trapped white ants, known as *ziisw*a, and some quails, which are very nutritious, and Kavosa would sell them at the market. During rainy season, there were several mushrooms that they could not eat all. She sold some at the markets.

Later, Kavosa discovered that there were better markets in Nakuru and Nairobi for everything she sold. In these big cities, people were tired of eating bread for breakfast and wanted different foodstuff. Kavosa started selling arrow roots, sweet potatoes, and cassava. She also sold maize and beans which were used to cook *amahengere*, which was a boiled mixture of maize and beans.

Kavosa did so well with her business that her family of three children her cousin Mideva lived comfortably. She was saving a lot of her profit for her children's tuition when they went to high school.

Kavosa may have been doing better financially, but she often stopped to think about her departed husband Musoda. She longingly thought about him. She wondered how he would react to the calls of his daughters when they called him "Baba." She never thought of replacing the love for him with another man. It was a promise she was willing to keep for as long as it took. She had started going to church, and one day the pastor talked about reunions with departed relatives. Kavosa was willing to wait until they reunited in the sweet repose of heaven. But she had things to do: raising the children Musoda left behind, and now she had acquired a nephew whom nobody wanted. She treated him like her own.

One rainy day in June, Kavosa was sitting in the living room talking to her lively children and telling them folk tales that she had heard from her own mother when something wet plopped onto her arm. She touched the spot with her forefinger and looked at it. It was a drop of rainwater, blackened by the soot from the old rafters. It struck Kavosa that her late mother's house was old now, and the roof was beginning to leak when it rained. It was small and grass -thatched. She wished she could transfer her big house in Masizi village to Gaago village but that was impossible. Musoda's mother would never let her, even if it were possible to transfer a house. Thinking aloud, a thought came to her mind—that she could actually afford to build one. She smiled.

The next time she went to Kisumu market, and after selling all her merchandise, she bought thirty corrugated iron sheets and brought them home in readiness to start construction of her semi-permanent house, like the one she had left behind. She had asked some boys in the village to help her ferry the iron sheets to the home. She had imagined that it was going to be as easy as building her late husband's house had been. What she had not reckoned with was the fact that she was an unmarried woman in her father's compound. Musoda had been a son of the home exercising his birthright. There was a world of difference.

Kavosa realized this when she went to ask her father to give her one tree for posts and all hell broke loose. Her step brothers would not let her build a house at her mother's home. Her father was frail and sickly but he also feared his unruly sons. The clan was not in favor of a girl building a house on her father's compound. They only said that it was taboo. The real reason must have been greed.

"We just let her stay here because she was still mourning her husband. It's time she should take back the children so she can get herself another husband," some clan members reiterated.

Kavosa and her family were given one week to find a place to live. She was no longer welcome in that home. Girls were not meant to be buried in their father's homesteads.

Villagers even started accusing her of arrogance because she had become rich and her children were better dressed. The children had started going to school and were performing extremely well. Kavosa would have to pull them out of school and move out of the home. She couldn't leave Mideva behind. She needed her.

Before the one-week deadline had elapsed, Kavosa traveled to Nairobi with her merchandise. After she sold everything, she asked a lady friend, who was one of her customers, if she could find a room somewhere to live with her children. The customer told her that she had a plot and, in fact, that same morning, one of her tenants had moved out. The plot was in Kangemi. Kavosa told her she would take the room even without thinking twice. She paid her six hundred Kenya shillings, which was enough for a month's rent and another month's rent in deposit. She traveled back home the following day and told Mideva that they were going to live in Nairobi.

Three days after the harassment, Kavosa and her family left the home. She would have loved to sell her iron sheets, but her step brothers wanted to keep them and threatened violence. She abandoned the idea and the next morning, they were on their way to Kangemi, Nairobi. Kavosa planned to support the family by still doing her business as long as Mideva took care of the children.

11

Iminza and Ajega were eight years old while Afandi was six years old when they transitioned to Nairobi. Life was quite different. They didn't have to go fetching water from a stream, but running water was on a faucet near the house. The school in which they were enrolled was also very close to the house. They no longer cooked food over open flames like back in the countryside, but they had a charcoal *jiko* and kerosene stove.

What they loved most was that they wore shoes and sweaters to school, something that was unheard of in country schools where they had started their schooling. They also had to adapt to learning in Swahili and English as opposed to Lurogoli, which they had spoken all the time both at school and home.

The two cousins, Kavosa and Mideva, continued to respect each other. Mideva was grateful that Kavosa had saved her from a life of turmoil and uncertainty. She had nowhere to live. Nobody seemed to care that it was not her fault that she couldn't bear children. Several husbands had used her, abused her, and sent her packing. Her brothers weren't sympathetic to her plight. All they wanted was to follow the tradition, which barred girls from living in their homes when they couldn't keep a marriage. They feared she might die in the home and be buried within the compound, which was taboo. In other cultures, such women were buried outside the fence of the compound to show that she didn't belong there.

Kavosa, on the other hand, was grateful that Mideva came home at an opportune time when she needed help. Her children were well taken care of. Kavosa didn't have to do any housework because it was all done by Mideva. Life was promising. In fact, Kavosa promised Mideva that they would stay together until God decided whatever He wanted with them.

It was as if God was listening in because a few months later, Mideva approached Kavosa and asked if she could sell some of the vegetables and fruits. "I'm sorry I have to ask you this, but it's just that I'm bored the whole day when the children go to school," she concluded. Kavosa was elated by the wisdom Mideva had. She offered to buy timber so they could construct a vegetable kiosk in front of their house.

Kavosa then started providing items for sale, one at a time, starting with *sukuma-wiki*. When they sold out, she brought onions and tomatoes as well as replenishing the *sukuma-wiki*. After one year of selling fruits and vegetables, Mideva realized customers bought produce from her but had to go elsewhere for salt and cooking fat. She introduced those items—then sugar and flour. By the end of two years, she had expanded her shop to accommodate even secondhand clothes. Kavosa got tired of having to get up at three o'clock in the morning to go to the market, and instead she took a job at Nairobi City Council. The City Council was hiring people to sweep the streets and keep the city clean. These new workers also planted and tended trees and flower gardens too. That was when Nairobi was still appropriately known as *The Green City in the Sun.*

It was while working for the Nairobi City Council that Kavosa heard about the houses at Jericho Estate being allocated to people who could afford to pay three hundred shillings in rent to the city council every year. She immediately went to apply for one and was lucky to get it. She was excited to break the news to the children and Mideva. However, Mideva declined to move in with her because of her flourishing business in Kanngemi. She begged Kavosa to let her stay because she didn't really need her. The children were grown and were about to finish in high school, except Afandi who was still in Form Two. Mideva had taught them to be responsible people. They could do all the house chore with ease.

For the first time since the two women got together to help each other out in Gaago village, they were emotionally parting ways. They wished each other well, as Kavosa piled some of her belongings on a hired truck to take to the other side of town, in Eastlands.

The teenage girls and boy were excited to find that the house was a permanent one, made of brick and cement. The floors were smooth, unlike the Kangemi houses, which had wooden walls and earthen floors. At Kangemi, one had to sprinkle water before sweeping to avoid dust. They had now come to live in a house that required them to mop, and to make matters better, the bathrooms and toilets were personal, meaning each house had its own bathroom and toilet. They didn't have to use stinky pit latrines with wooden walls and iron sheets any more. They were a class higher.

Life in Jericho was different from the life the kids were used to. They made new friends who knew more things than them. For example, they knew some music and dance moves that Iminza and Afandi wished they knew too. Iminza made friends with other girls in Jericho, who introduced her to boyfriends. She was in her final year in high school when she got pregnant. Her mother had witnessed her throwing up every morning and decided to take her to the dispensary to see if it was malaria. The nurse pronounced her pregnant. Kavosa was disappointed but calmly asked who was responsible. She gave the name of the boy as Manoah, a young man that lived in the block of flats nearby, whom everyone called "Manosh." Kavosa asked to see him, and Iminza agreed to ask him to come and see her.

One Saturday when Kavosa was off duty, Manosh sent word that he was ready to pay her a visit. He indeed came to Jericho accompanied by his friend and an uncle, just to show the seriousness of the matter. After they sat down and were served tea and *mandazi*, which Iminza had learned to make very well, the uncle was the one who spoke. He said they had come to confirm that Iminza's "luggage"—as Maragolis euphemistically refer to pregnancy—was theirs. They had come to take "their wife" home so that all the responsibility of hospital bills would be theirs. Anything else like dowry discussion had to wait until Iminza "untied herself," meaning until she gave birth to a baby.

Kavosa called Iminza aside and asked her if she was sure she wanted this. She said she did because she was already pregnant and that she was lucky Manoah had accepted the responsibility. Kavosa recalled a neighbor's daughter who had died trying to abort through dubious means because the boyfriend had dumped her. Kavosa felt lucky that they were discussing this. She had no objection, although she really wanted Iminza to finish high school and get a job.

After two weeks, Kavosa called Mideva from Kangemi, plus another friend of hers and Afandi, and sent them to escort Iminza to her husband's house in East Leigh. She knew this was a better arrangement and quite different from her own marriage to Musoda. She didn't go with the group because the culture didn't allow her to. It should be known that even when a girl wedded, her parents wouldn't attend the wedding. They would only throw a party for the girl and villagers, and then stayed behind, as a group of women go to the wedding, singing songs in praise of their daughter.

It took Kavosa quite some time to get used to the idea that Iminza was now married. But she still had Ajega and Afandi in her Jericho house. Ajega performed very well in his School Certificate Examination, and he joined Form Five and Six after which he sat for the Higher School Certificate.

Afandi's was a different story all together. She had been in Form Two when Iminza got pregnant and subsequently got married to the man responsible for the pregnancy. Iminza had been Afandi's role model. She copied everything Iminza did. If Kavosa bought a dress for Iminza, Afandi would cry for the same. At first, she didn't do very well in school but seeing her sister come home with presents for being first in her class made her work so hard that she also started excelling in class.

When Iminza got pregnant, she cried. When she moved to live with her husband, Afandi cried even more. On several occasions, she would refused to do any house chores. Kavosa had to do everything. Ajega was always busy, explaining that, "Higher schools required loads of studying.".

At the tender age of fourteen, Afandi started disappearing from home without telling anybody where she went. She would stay the whole day and came back late in the evening, going straight to her room. She wouldn't answer questions from her mother or Ajega. Later, she graduated from staying days and would be gone for days and nights. Iminza was called upon by her mother to come and talk to her sister, but Afandi's answer was a question: "Who asked you how you got pregnant?'

Afandi's character changed completely. Her mother meted out corporal punishment in vain. At one point, she sought the help of the police. Afandi was dragged to the police station and locked in a cell for two days. She cried and begged, promising never to repeat her mistakes. On her release, she only stayed home for two weeks and then she was gone. This time she stayed away for a period of three years, during which time people came up with theories. Some said she died, others said she had joined a brothel. Other people said she had gone to Mombasa to do prostitution. Mombasa, being a leading tourist destination in Kenya, has a lot going on.

As it were, this was the closest to the truth. Afandi had joined a group of girls in the estate, who like her, quit school and used to go to town to learn "funky dancing," as they called it. They had been recruited by a certain woman who operated a brothel. After dancing, they would be introduced to customers, who paid hefty sums of money to the lady. But the lady would pay these girls a mere two hundred shillings a week. The police raided this place quite often, but the lady would grease their palms to look aside, and the business continued. Another woman in the business had stolen some of the girls and transported them to Mombasa, promising more money. Afandi was one of them.

This story was later related by one of the girls who finally got away from that kind of business and came home to repent to her parents. She even changed her ways and begged to go back to school. This happened after she had been given away to a client who finished with her and offered her to his dog. She was forced to do things which only wild animals could do. She was threatened by the white client not to scream but let his dog "enjoy" her. She left the hotel room crying and being warned never to tell anybody or else she would be shot dead.

The only safe place this girl had to go to was her parents' house, to apologize. She was forgiven and taken back in. She went back to school, studied hard, and later became a lawyer. All the time, she had the abuse on her mind and wanted to help some of the girls still being exploited at a tender age.

Afandi never turned back. She only came home after three years and said she was now too used to her type of lifestyle to change. Asked what she did, Afandi avoided the question and said that she worked in Mombasa and it was nobody's business to "know" what she did.

While Iminza was happily married and having children, Afandi was behaving like a world tourist. She'd hook up with a man who would take her places, and after a short while there would be another man in the picture. She even travelled to Germany with one man, but she left the man and got herself a younger one. The older man nearly killed her when she fled back to Kenya.

Afandi would steal money from a man's pockets while he slept and run away. Kavosa would never touch any of her daughter's ill-gotten money. She worked hard at her job, and soon found a better job as a subordinate staff member at Kenyatta National Hospital. She was happy with the new job. She thought that Iminza was married and gone, Afandi had become wayward, but she thanked God for Ajega, a boy who would take care of her in old age. That was a general belief among the Maragoli.

Ajega was good at his studies, and Kavosa worked hard to provide whatever he needed. She took out loans from her job's cooperative societies to pay his tuition so he didn't have to be sent home from school. Ajega was very appreciative of his mother's efforts. Although Kavosa was in actuality his aunt, he didn't know of any other parent apart from Kavosa, whom he called "Mama" and loved very much. Like Kavosa, Ajega was very disappointed when Afandi dropped out of school to start a dubious type of life. He had hoped the girls would join hands with him to work hard at school and later get jobs to sustain their mother. She needed a rest, as she had worked too hard to provide for them.

Ajega went on to finish his Higher School Certificate successfully and was admitted at Nairobi University to pursue a degree in commerce. Still, his mother, Kavosa, a Standard Three dropout, made sure that she sustained his education. She understood the importance of education and wished she had been allowed to go to school during her time. She grew up when importance was placed on male children, as they took over the leadership of homesteads after their fathers. It was believed that female children would get married and raise children in another clan. But she was still grateful that

God had given her a brain for business and later gave her a job even if she barely knew how to read and write.

Ajega, her "last" child, became her focal point. She made sure she took loans to pay his university tuition. Ajega didn't at one time take the HELB (Higher Education Loans Board) loans. His tuition was paid up front by his Kavosa. Those who didn't know the story behind Ajega just knew him as Kavosa's biological son. Very few people associated him with his long-lost father and mother. He didn't even know them or have a picture of them in his mind. He was too young when Kavosa rescued him from malnutrition and jiggers. She took good care of him. She wanted the best for him and so far, she had achieved it as far as education was concerned.

When Ajega eventually graduated, the search for a job started. He had passed his examinations well and graduated with an Upper Second Class Bachelor's honors degree in commerce. Job opportunities at the time were numerous for those who had education. The government wanted him, banks wanted him, and some private hospital offered him a job, but he chose to work for a large insurance company in order to use his accounting option of the commerce degree. The company was an international one, and Ajega was delighted to be associated with it.

Kavosa was so happy when she came home from work to the news that Ajega had gotten a job. He showed her the offer letter, but it was in English. Kavosa could only read and write Kimaragoli, and a little Swahili, as the alphabet was nearly the same. However, Ajega read the letter and translated it for her.

He had three days in which to get a medical examination. Kavosa also used the three days to find money to buy her son a nice suit so he would look presentable at his first job. This was done on their way back from hospital where Kavosa worked, which also happened to be where she had taken Ajega for a medical examination. She had taken Ajega to some of the doctors she knew personally, for introduction. She didn't mince her words but proudly announced that Ajega was her son and had completed university education and gotten a job. She earned many people's admiration because even those placed highly in society could sometimes fail to educate their children that far.

As much as Kavosa regretted the idea that she was denied an education to pave the way for her brother, she still raised her son like the typical male child. Ajega couldn't cook, wash clothes, do dishes or go to the market in the presence of his mother and sisters. He only started to learn to cook when his sister Iminza got married and Afandi quit school to go into prostitution; and sometimes when his mother was too busy to cook. They lived, just the two of them, but Kavosa would do all the laundry and house cleaning. Those were jobs for women.

Whenever Kavosa wasn't working, she would go to do a little buying and selling of vegetables at the market, just to make some extra money. This meant that Ajega needed to cook and save some food for his mother. Ajega, who wasn't used to doing those chores, thought it was too hard on him.

It was on one of the days Kavosa went to the market after work. She came back home at seven o'clock in the evening and before opening the door, she was surprised to hear a woman's voice in the house. She wondered who it could be and hoped Afandi had come to visit—or was it Iminza? But she also wondered why Iminza would be at her house at that late hour because her husband never allowed her and his children to spend nights elsewhere.

Kavosa inserted the key in the lock and turned it. The door clicked open. Sitting on the same old couch with Ajega was a short brown girl of about twenty-two years of age. She had her braided hair tied into a pony tail. She was holding a baby girl that was about one year old. When Kavosa came in, Ajega jumped to his feet and introduced her as Sophia, and the little girl's name was Carol. He added without hesitating, "I have taken her in to be my wife."

To say Kavosa was shocked is an understatement. She felt anger welling up inside her but suppressed it instantly by politely saying to Sophia, "Welcome to our house, and I hope you will like it here," as she took the food she was carrying to the kitchen. She summoned Ajega to follow her to the kitchen, where she asked him if the baby was his and why he hadn't said anything before.

Ajega honestly told his mother that he had been watching how hard Sophia worked in a neighbor's house as a housemaid. She got pregnant by the man of the house where she worked and so the man sent her away before his wife discovered the relationship.

"She will tell you he whole story if you ask her, but I have been talking to her secretly for over three months now."

Apparently, Ajega had admired how hard Sophia worked in a neighbor's hose. He wanted somebody to do the same work in their house so he didn't have to do the chores. At the same time, he empathized with Sophia's problems since she was young. Instinctively, he was trying to save somebody's life the way his was saved.

The following day was a Saturday, and Kavosa didn't want to go to the market. She wanted to stay home and get to know this strange girl her son had brought into the house as a wife.

Sophia explained to Kavosa that her life was a nightmare. She had been born in Tigoi Village of a single mother who died in childbirth. She never got to know her mother or her father. She was raised by her grandmother, who was very nice to her, but her uncles and their wives mistreated her very much. Her grandmother enrolled her in school, but her uncles would fetch her out of school to come home and run errands for them, or just watch their children. Her grandmother was overpowered by her sons. There was nothing she could do but pray.

Then, one day when Sophia was sixteen years old, a lady in the village who saw her problems after her grandmother died took her to Nairobi to be a housemaid. The first people she worked for were very nice, and she stayed with them for four years. When the last of their children started school, they didn't need a maid any longer. They handed her over to another couple.

The woman was very abusive, but Sophia persevered because she didn't have anywhere else to go. While the woman was hard to please, the man was kind and treated her as a human being. Whenever the man defended her against his wife, the wife accused him of having an affair with her. Sophia was young and naïve and didn't even know what the woman meant. She had never been with a man, and so she didn't know how those in an affair behaved.

As much as the woman abused her, she was grateful to have a roof over her head, until one day when the wife visited the village, leaving Sophia with her husband and children behind. She had gone to attend a relative's burial and would be back after a week. The first three days were good, but the fourth day would haunt her forever. The man dropped the children at school as he headed to work—or so Sophia believed. She embarked on her house chores as usual but was surprised to see her boss's husband drive back by ten o'clock. She thought he had forgotten something. He went straight to the bedroom and called out to Sophia to get him a glass of water as he had a headache. Sophia who was scrubbing the bathroom ran to the kitchen and washed her hands before retrieving a clean glass from the wall unit. She got a bottle of water from the fridge and innocently took the glass of water to his boss's bedroom.

As she handed the glass to him, he went past the glass and grabbed her hand. "Do not scream otherwise you will explain to my wife what you were doing in my bedroom when I am here," he said. Sophia feared his wife very much because of her temper and abusive language. She was between a rock and a hard place. He pulled her to the bed, ripped her clothes and hungrily feasted on her young body like a hyena. That was the day Sophia lost her virginity and got pregnant.

The man dressed up and went back to work. Sophia remained, feeling empty, guilty, and dejected. The man warned her never to say anything. By the time the wife came, she noticed that something was amiss with Sophia. When asked, Sophia could only say that she was sick. After two months, Sophia was still sick and throwing up a lot. The woman fired her, saying she couldn't keep feeding an ever-ailing person. She then moved from house to house wherever she could find accommodations until a well-wisher saw her pregnancy and helped her with a place to stay until she had her baby.

She wished her grandmother was still alive so she could go live with her. She even tried to go back to the village, but her uncles said they couldn't afford to feed another mouth. So, it was at this well-wisher's house that Ajega saw her running errands with a baby on her back.

She walked with the speed of lightning and worked with such expertise. She never seemed to get tired working with a baby on her back. The first day he greeted her he fell in love with her musical voice. He made a habit of walking by her house on his way from work just to see her. Sophia was first apprehensive when Ajega told her he loved her and wanted her for a wife. She didn't trust men since the case that gave her the burden of a baby, although she loved Carol very much.

Sophia talked to her well-wisher about Ajega wanting to marry her. The well-wisher, having no immediate plans with her, encouraged her to look into the matter. Although Ajega didn't confide in his mother about Sophia, he believed that all would be well. That Friday was the day he decided to take her home as a wife.

Kavosa listened to Sophia's story with empathy, thinking of her own life. She would have preferred an educated wife for Ajega, but he had made his choice. She wasn't going to interfere. All she wanted was the happiness of her son. She knew that was the only person that would take care of her in old age. Her culture demanded so.

13

Ajega was an educated man with a prestigious job, but he chose to take in Sophia, a poor homeless girl with her baby girl who hardly went to school because her maternal uncles never let her. She was treated in the home like a slave. Her grandmother, who was old and frail watched helplessly, wishing Sophia's mother hadn't died giving birth. She had been raped by her boss's husband, which resulted in pregnancy. Ajega didn't let her bad experiences deter him. In Sophia he saw a beautiful, submissive girl who would make a very good wife. Moreover, she was a very hard worker. She never complained about anything. She would work with her baby on the back.

Ajega was now relieved that he could no longer do the house chores after work. He had brought in somebody who knew how to do it. He was also thinking of how he could relieve his mother of the big burden of coming from work and having to do housework. He thought that had he married a woman with the same education as he, there would be arguments in the house all the time. He had witnessed his friend Tom, who was a year ahead of him at the university, who married a classmate. They were always fighting as to who was boss in the house. Ajega hoped for a woman who would respect his mother, and in Sophia, he got one.

Ajega and Sophia came to know each other better as days went by, relating their respective stories. Ajega said he didn't know much about his biological parents and that he was grateful to have an aunt—*mother*—who loved him unconditionally.

Apart from developing love for each other, Ajega developed a special bond with Sophia's baby, Carol. As soon as he got home from work, he took Carol to play with. He went everywhere with her. He was the one who fed her. He became a very good parent to Carol, who called him "father" and Sophia found relief at least for someone to hold Carol while she did her work. Kavosa also loved Carol, who called her "Guku," which means grandmother.

Sophia didn't want to be a simple housewife. She asked to do what Mideva had done in Kangemi. She asked for a little capital to buy fruits and vegetables to sell during the day. She built a wooden kiosk next to their house and started selling fruits like paw paws, avocados, pineapples, pears, plums, oranges, and limes. She sold vegetables like carrots, kale, cabbage, onions, tomatoes, and broccoli. She was good at dealing with customers, and so, before long, she was very well-known in the estate.

She would get up very early in the morning to prepare her items for sale before coming back home to prepare breakfast for her husband and mother-in-law before they went to work. She would then spend the whole day selling her wares. This way, she made money and also saved on food funds, as they would no longer have to buy produce. They just ate whatever hadn't been sold the previous day.

At the age of fifty-five, Kavosa had to retire from government service because that was the retirement age in Kenya. While she waited for her retirement dues, which took as long as two years, she joined Sophia in the fruit and vegetable business. It was a happy family. Carol grew like a weed, and just as if the years were flying, she was soon in school and doing very well. Sophia and Ajega had since gotten two boys. The first boy was ten years younger than his sister Carol, while the younger boy came two years later. Ajega loved his sons very much, but many would notice that he loved Carol more. A commonly-held belief was that daughters were always closer to their fathers while boys get attached to their mothers.

When Carol eventually joined one of the prestigious high schools in Western Kenya, Ajega would always want to be the one to take Carol to school. He would give an excuse that his wife and mother were too busy with the business to take Carol to school. The women thought it good that Ajega was doing all the traveling. Ajega would travel all the way to see Carol during her school's Visiting Days. He would buy her nice things and always gave her more pocket money than the rest of the children.

School girls were not allowed to wear home clothes while at school, but at the last day of the school term of the school Ajega would drive all the way to Western Kenya to pick Carol up from school. He didn't want her to travel by public means like other girls. He would buy her fine clothes and carry them to school so Carol could dress well as they traveled back to Nairobi. He didn't want to torture his daughter to wear school uniform when holidays had started was his explanation.

During school holidays, twice a week, Carol would go to her father's office just to have lunch with him. Ajega made sure she had fare to town and back. Otherwise, she sat in the office until the close of the day so they could ride back home together.

Carol didn't have many friends. Most of her leisure time was occupied with her father. They jogged together, ate together, went shopping together, and sat watching television together. Both Sophia and Kavosa attributed it to the education they shared, which the two of them did not have. But Kavosa, being wise as she was, had sensed that something was awry.

Meanwhile, after Kavosa got her retirement dues, she discussed it with Ajega and agreed that she would invest in land. She bought a five-acre plot of land in Kapsabet Nandi, a fertile place that did well in the growing of maize, beans, tea, and all sorts of vegetables. She knew she was buying the land for Ajega because boys inherit land from their parents but her brothers had sold most of their land in Gaago after their father died. She didn't want to leave Ajega without a home when God called her. In the back of her head, she knew that Afandi would come back in her old age and would need a place to call home. She put up a small house on the land in which anybody visiting could sleep in. Her plan was to have Ajega save enough money to construct a more permanent and modern house.

Before the big house was constructed, both Kavosa and Sophia loved to visit the village and simply enjoyed the scenery and the fresh air, which was different from the city air. They would go to the village in turns, but when schools were closed, both women would take the boys to the village, leaving Ajega and Carol in Nairobi. They would stay for a whole month, and sometimes Kavosa would stay in the village for up to three months before going back to Nairobi

Kavosa was a member of women groups in Nairobi. While on one of these trips to her rural home, she remembered she needed to attend a crucial meeting to discuss how to collect money from members who had absconded with loans. She needed to travel to Nairobi on short notice. She boarded a shuttle from Kapsabet town at a late hour, arriving in Nairobi at around eight o'clock. She then took a bus to Jericho, and since she had a spare key to the house, she didn't feel the need to knock. Upon opening the door, she was shocked to find Ajega lying half naked on the couch while Carol was massaging his chest. They both jumped at the sight of her. "What do you think you are doing?!" she demanded. Ajega knew that he had been cornered by his mother. Carol was the one who talked. "Daddy has a cold so he asked me to apply some cough rub on his chest. Kavosa was infuriated. It was an abomination, but Ajega assured her that nothing happened. She wasn't fully convinced but gave her the benefit of the doubt.

From this time on, Kavosa kept a close eye on the two. She would always wonder why Ajega let his daughter touch his bare chest. She may not have been his biological child, but according to the Maragoli tradition, one's mother's husband became his or her father, and a father's wife automatically became one's mother.

All half-brothers and half-sisters are one's siblings. In blended families, the children from either side became brothers and sisters. Any sexual relation between any two of those is considered incestuous. It would call for a cleansing, which involved banishment. Kavosa was worried for her son, who had become hers because she raised and educated him.

The thought that Ajega and Carol could be having a sexual relationship was too big a burden for Kavosa to carry. She was stressed all the time, which manifested in ailments that couldn't otherwise be explained. She had a persistent headache that never seemed to ease, even when she took medication. She couldn't bring herself to tell anybody what she had witnessed—not even Sophia. It would be gossip. She had to wait and see more if there was anything else to come.

Meanwhile, Ajega wouldn't eat unless Carol was seated beside him. He would be stroking her hair with his left hand as he ate with his right one. Kavosa would pretend to be asleep on the couch as she watched them through her fingers that covered her face as she lay on a couch. The two would be duped that she was asleep and exchange glances and sometimes a quick kiss. Kavosa would feel her stomach revolting to the point of throwing up, but for some reason she needed more evidence.

All this while, Sophia was in the village with the two boys. As it were, Sophia had noticed the dubious behavior a while ago and had confronted her husband, but he denied everything. That's when she decided to move to the village because her husband had transferred his love to his stepdaughter, something that was taboo in Maragoli communities. Sophia didn't confide in anybody—not even Kavosa. She had no parents to complain to. She feared that she might be sent away from the marriage so she could resume her life of vagrancy. She was a survivor and she was good at perseverance.

And so, the days passed.

C arol eventually became so sick that she couldn't eat. She puked every time she drank water and became so dehydrated that Kavosa decided to take her to the doctor. On thorough examination, the doctor pronounced her two months pregnant.

Weeks earlier she had moved from the bedroom that she shared with Kavosa to sleep on the floor in the living room. The reasons she gave were that she felt hot in the bedroom and wanted to sleep on the cool floor. Although Kavosa would occasionally tiptoe to the living room to see if Carol was on her makeshift sleeping place on the floor, for the first few days she saw her peacefully asleep. It turns out that it was a mere tactic to dupe Kavosa make here believe that nothing was going on because they suspected that she was watching them. After one week, Carol wasn't on the floor. It would be neatly made as the previous evening like it hadn't been slept in.

One night, Kavosa decided to sit and wait to see from where Carol would emerge. She sat on her made bedding on the floor and waited nearly the whole night. Early in the morning just before sunrise Carol slipped out of Ajega's bedroom, hoping to sleep in her bed only to find Kavosa sitting in it.

Without being asked Carol began explaining that, "Daddy just called me five minutes ago to massage his chest."

Kavosa answered, sternly. "I wasn't born yesterday. I have been sitting here the whole night," she said honestly. "Do you think what you are doing with your mother's husband is right? This is your father. Did you ever go to school with boys of your age?" she asked with a lot of bitterness.

Carol remained quiet. But Ajega emerged from the bedroom with only a boxer shorts on and came in defense of Carol.

Kavosa behaved as a grown woman and played it cool. She intended to call Sophia from the village and two elderly men from the Vaguuga clan to come to Nairobi and render a decision on what had befallen her family. She knew it was taboo.

Later that morning, Kavosa went to the Post Office Savings bank and withdrew some money and wired it home for Sophia to come to Nairobi. She also wired some money to Gaago for Ayuya and Esabu to come to Nairobi and figure out what to do. It was while awaiting their arrival that Carol became sick, and the doctor pronounced her pregnant. It was Kavosa's duty to interview her before the elders arrived. Carol had no way but to declare her stepfather, Ajega as the owner of the pregnancy. Although Kavosa knew it all along, this confirmation nearly killed her. Her blood pressure soared. She started getting nosebleeds, but she refused to be touched or be taken to hospital by Ajega. Although a neighbor came to her rescue by rushing her to the doctor, Kavosa didn't disclose her source of pain and stress. She eagerly waited for the team from the village.

Ayuya and Esabu were the elders of Kavosa's clan who dealt with all cultural matters, from funerals to dowry negotiations to taboo relations. Kavosa went to pick them up from the railway station on a Saturday morning, knowing that was the day Ajega would be at home. They still didn't know why their daughter had called them from the village to the city, and neither did Ajega nor Carol know of their coming.

It was therefore a surprise to see them enter the house. Ajega hadn't been to Gaago village for a long time, and so he didn't know who they were. The moment they came in, Kavosa summoned everybody to come to the living room. The old men had to do their work before washing their hands, according to the tradition.

As soon as everyone was seated, Kavosa stood up and introduced each person. Pointing to Ajega, she said, "This is Ajega, the son of my brother who disappeared into the sisal plantation farms and never came back home. We don't even know if his mother is alive or dead because I never saw her. He is the same boy I rescued from jiggers and kwashiorkor as you all know."

Ajega had never known that Kavosa was not his mother but an aunt. She loved him too much to have been a mere aunt. She educated him up to the university level without having taken out a loan from HELB. It was all so hard to comprehend.

While he was still deep in thought, Kavosa was introducing Sophia. "She is his wife. She has two very nice boys with him. Her name is Sophia. She had to go to my farm in Kapsabet because Ajega wasn't treating her well. He had found himself another woman whom he loved more than the mother of his sons."

At this point, Esabu, the short-tempered one, asked where the woman was.

"The woman is this one seated here," Kavosa answered as she pointed to Carol. "The biggest problem is that Carol is the daughter of Sophia. She came here with her when she was a year old. Ajega raised her as his daughter, but now things have changed. She is his new wife, and as we speak, she is pregnant," she concluded.

The clan elders knew exactly what to do. Banishment was the punishment meted out to such people. Immediately, they ordered Ajega to get out of the house and get lost like his father. He was to take his new wife with him and never come back to the family. He had lost all rights as a son of Vaguuga clan. He was not supposed to interact with any family member, and he was immediately to get going, taking Carol with him.

Ajega tried to argue and even called the police. Unfortunately, the policeman who came over also understood the situation's taboo nature. He said he couldn't do anything about a clan feud. He walked away as crowds gathered to ridicule Carol for allowing her father to sleep with her. The crowds also cursed Ajega for doing an abominable thing, making his daughter pregnant. The crowds, who mostly were neighbors and knew Kavosa very well as a respectable woman, were even ready to die for her. They assisted in throwing Ajega's and Carol's belongings out of the house and escorting them as they left shamefully. It was quite a spectacle.

The clan elders prepared some cleansing concoction. They mixed it in a basin full of water and sprinkled it around the whole house. They pronounced curses on Carol and Ajega never to see light in their lives, but to live in the darkness they had brought to the clan. They made a charcoal fire and burned some medicine on it to scare off the evil spirits that were brought to the house through incest.

It was after they were satisfied that the job was well done that they sat down to wash their hands and have some food.

Ajega and Carol were now homeless. Ajega was used to depending on his "mother,", so much that he never thought of finding his own place to live. He had been thrown out of the house and with an immediate burden: a pregnant wife. The first thing he did was to run as fast as he could, away from the crowd that was screaming at him and baying for his blood. The next stop was a cheap hotel on River Road in Nairobi. They checked into a room and would stay for seven months.

A pregnant wife living in filthy hotel conditions was unbearable for Ajega. Moreover, they had been living on his savings until they were completely dwindled. The events of that Saturday morning had never left Ajega's mind. He regretted his actions that had disrupted his life, but it was too late now. He would never reclaim his place in the clan after what he did.

The stress that came with the banishment affected his work performance. He would go to work late and leave early. He started to see Carol as a burden and not a wife. He yearned for his mother's love. He started imagining Sophia as his ideal wife, but she was now out of reach.

Carol's day of delivery came, and she started having contractions. She had prolonged labor, but she wasn't dilating as was supposed to be. Ajega, having been out of work for several months and having lived on his savings to pay hotel bills and eating in restaurants every day, was left dead broke. He couldn't afford the hospital bill—not even the taxi to take Carol to a maternity hospital. It was Carol's screams that attracted a hotel attendant to the room. Some years past a woman had been discovered in the same hotel strangled to death by a man she had been frequenting the hotel with. The hotel workers had to be vigilant and extra careful about their guests.

When the hotel attendant banged on the door, a dazed Ajega opened the door. The first thing the hotel worker saw was blood on the floor. He immediately called the manager who called a taxi to rush Carol to Pumwani Maternity Hospital. On arrival at the hospital, Carol was wheeled into the theatre for a caesarian section, but she didn't make it out of the anesthesia. She died on the operating table because it was too late. The baby boy survived for a few hours, but due to prolonged labor, he too was too exhausted to survive. He also died.

Ajega had no money to bury his wife and child. He yearned for the help of his mother even more. He knew she always knew what to do, but he had burned the bridge between his mother and him—and also his wife Sophia.

In order to get rid of him, the hotel management, where he had lived for a year, offered to help bury his wife and child on condition that he didn't return to stay at the hotel. He had no money to pay for his room anyway.

Carol and her baby boy were buried at Langata Cemetery with no ceremony, no church service or requiem mass, no flowers, and no hymns. It was so sad. But Ajega went back to the hotel and kept dodging the authority for another three months, making it a year since they had left Jericho. Ajega became a beggar. Those who saw him emaciated knew that the curses pronounced against him had taken root.

15

Ajega had been begging for several months since the death of Carol. Like the proverbial prodigal son in the Bible, he finally decided to go back home to Kavosa's house in Jericho although he suspected that there wasn't going to be any fatted calf for him. He walked a distance of about six miles from the Nairobi city center to Jericho, arriving tired, thirsty, and hungry. His feet were so dusty that he looked like he was wearing brown socks. He had sold all his clothes in order to sustain his standard of living. The tattered clothes he was wearing were his only worldly possessions.

Kavosa was at home when Ajega came knocking, but she couldn't let him into the house. He had been banished by the clan forever for sleeping with his step-daughter. That was an unforgivable sin in Maragoli tradition. There was no way Ajega could be accepted back into the clan. His fate was sealed, just like when Cain killed his brother in the Bible and was sent away from the home he knew.

Ajega believed and hoped that his desperation would touch his mother's heart, but it didn't. Kavosa knew what was right from wrong according to the tradition. The only rule she broke was when she ran away from being officially inherited when she was clearly still mourning her husband. She knew all the other traditions and adhered to them. She could not therefore allow a cursed person into her house and her life again. She had done all she could for Ajega to have a good life, but he had turned his life inside out.

Kavosa screamed for help when Ajega tried to force himself into the house that he knew very well. Jericho was full of curious idlers who would rush to any scene within seconds. People knew and respected Kavosa. They also knew that Ajega had broken the hand that raised him. He was now man enough to fend for himself.

The crowd gathered. People were asking what was going on and others giving conflicting answers because they didn't really know what was going on. They saw Ajega looking like a madman and some wanted to lynch him. They were all just waiting for someone to shout, "Thief," so they could all pounce on him, but nobody did. Some even pitied him when they recognized him as the son of Kavosa who had attended Nairobi University and had found a nice job with an insurance company. "Surely people change," one woman was heard saying.

Among the people in the crowd was Njoroge. Njoroge was a charcoal dealer who didn't have a house but had constructed a cardboard shack near his heap of charcoal sacks that he was selling. He forced his way through the crowd and went to Ajega who was sitting down on the ground, his face bowed in shame. He took him by the hand and led him away. He only uttered one sentence: "Do unto others what you would want done to you," sounding like the local pastor, although Njoroge never went to church. In fact, he had been accused many times for selling marijuana to the local boys, who ended up dropping out of school.

Njoroge was not a Maragoli but belonged to the Kikuyu tribe. Many of his tribesmen bragged about having few constraints as far as culture was concerned. Word had it that a Kikuyu man could impregnate his daughter and still raise the child together with his other children. Some actually laughed at Maragolis for sending away such children who were products of incest. And for Ajega's story, they reasoned that he and Carol didn't have blood relations and so it could not be referred to as incest.

Njoroge himself had been accused in the past of luring young children to his shack and defiling them, but nobody had ever caught him red-handed. In Ajega he found a friend and one who would help him deliver his charcoal by bicycle to whoever bought a sack. Most people would just buy small tins at retail price. Njoroge had just saved Ajega from a potential lynching. But he had bigger plans in mind.

Ajega was given a dish of *githeri*, which is a boiled mixture of maize and beans, and a cup of tea from a nearby kiosk that served as a restaurant, paid for by Njoroge, He also offered Ajega a place to sleep.

For several months Ajega could be seen ferrying charcoal and looking even dirtier. But at least he had a place to sleep and a job that paid him enough to pay for his food at the kiosk. Every day he passed by Kavosa's house and stared in disbelief that he now lived in a shack while the house he grew up in was here and had enough room.

He would go and discuss it with Njoroge, who also needed a house to live in. Possibly if Ajega got the house he would move in with him. He made a point of taking Ajega to an estate officer and lied to him that Kavosa had denied her son entry into the house. The estate *officer* asked them to prove that the house was Ajega's and that Kavosa was snatching it from him. They went back to their shack and doubled their effort of vending their charcoal to raise enough money for their cause.

They took some money and bribed the estate officer so he would rule the case in their favor. He accepted the bribe because he was in need of money to pay for his son's tuition. Instead of giving them actual documents, the estate officer faked papers and gave fake ownership to Ajega.

16

I t was Monday afternoon, and Kavosa, who had resumed her small-scale selling of fruits and vegetables, had just left her kiosk to go to the house for lunch. As she opened her door and ventured inside, she was startled to see a man enter the house after her. Before she could scream, the man held her and covered her mouth with his dirty palm. It was Ajega. He ordered her to vacate the house in silence, as it now belonged to him—otherwise she would regret it.

They argued, with Kavosa asking him to respect her as his mother and Ajega shouting about why she had let him live a sorry life.

"I did everything for you so you could have a better life than me," she said. "All my life has been an uphill struggle. I hoped you would ease my pain," she added.

They struggled as Ajega tried to throw his mother out of the house, but Kavosa wasn't letting go. She screamed, and because Ajega knew the screams would mean danger to him, he beat her up. He punched Kavosa, boxed her, twisted her hands, and kicked her. Finally, he grabbed a rolling pin and tried to knock her on her head with it. Kavosa avoided the hit by shielding herself with her arm. With all his might Ajega struck the arm with the roller. There was a loud crack as the bone broke.

Ajega got scared when he saw his mother's hand dangling, held by the skin. The pain Kavosa felt went through her whole body. She gave one scream and then passed out. Neighbors rushed in to help. They frog marched Ajega to the chief's office.

Kavosa sat down by the roadside, her broken arm dangling by the skin, unable to cry. The pain was excruciating, and the cause of the pain was even more painful. She was in Jericho Estate, Nairobi, surrounded by idle people. Anything happening, no matter how small, attracted throngs of spectators. However, this was no small matter. People had been lynched for less. It was called "mob justice"—the only kind of justice that the people who meted it out knew.

The questions people asked were manifold: Who had done this? Why would one do such a thing to a seventy-six-year old woman? But Kavosa was in too much pain to answer, her heart full of regrets.

The neighbors took charge of the house to made sure that Ajega or "that stupid Njoroge" didn't come inside.

It took Kavosa six months to regain usage of her hand, which had been in a cast all that time. Unfortunately, at the time, most police officers were men, and few case against men would see the light of day. When Kavosa was well enough to follow up the matter with the police, the answer was, "That's a domestic affair." Kavosa left it to her God.

Knowledgeable people advised her to solve the case of the house by going to the city council offices. That was when she discovered that Ajega had forged papers for the ownership of her house. To solve the case once and for all, the same estate officer asked Kavosa if she would switch houses with someone else in the neighboring Jerusalem Estate who wanted to move to Jericho.

That is what happened, and that's what saved Kavosa from losing her city council house. The houses were relatively inexpensive and could be passed on from one generation to the next as long as the city council rent was paid. The house Kavosa and Ajega were fighting for was now occupied by a different person. Her broken bones and heart had healed and it was time to move again. That was what she had done all her life. The cultural wisdom and mindset that had her set her expectations on her son had turned out to be her worst nightmare. When it came down to it, she had capably taken care of herself, and she would keep doing so until...

THE END